SEDUCED
at
SUNSET

SEDUCED
at
SUNSET

Julianne MacLean

Cover Design: The Killion Group
Editor: Patricia Thomas

Formatting: Hale Author Services

Part One

A Kiss Before the Wedding

One

June 12, 1842

*T*HOUGH SHE WAS YOUNG—only one month shy of her nineteenth year—Lady Adelaide Robins possessed the wisdom to understand that certain moments in one's life were turning points that could never be undone.

This, she knew, was one of those moments.

Years from now, she would look back on the choice she had made this evening as she sat at her desk, quill in hand, and wonder, what if I had acted differently? What if I had never written this letter?

Lady Adelaide did not know if she was making the right decision tonight. How could she? She did not possess a crystal ball, nor the life experience to judge most men of the world.

Except, perhaps, for one man, who was very dear to her heart.

William Thomas, her friend since childhood, was the second son of a viscount, while she was the daughter of an earl, raised on a vast estate in Yorkshire with her two older sisters, who were now married.

Their father was thankful for the husbands her sisters had procured, for it was common knowledge that their family was impoverished, and there was no money for dowries. Not a single farthing.

Nevertheless, Mary and Margarite had married well, which was no great surprise, for they were widely regarded as incomparable beauties.

Margarite had married the handsome eldest son of a baron from the south who would inherit his father's prosperous estate one day, while Mary had wed a less handsome but exceedingly amiable youngest son of a marquess, who was a well-loved vicar in Devonshire.

Now it was Adelaide's turn to walk down the aisle, and her father was beside himself with joy, for she had done better than both her sisters. Somehow, against all likelihood, and without intent, she had captured the heart of a duke.

Not just any duke, mind you. Adelaide was now famously engaged to Theodore Sinclair—His Grace, the Duke of Pembroke—one of the highest ranking peers in the realm, wealthy beyond any imaginings, impossibly handsome of course, and with a palace considered to be one of England's greatest architectural achievements. It was an extravagant baroque masterpiece with splendid Italian Gardens (recently designed by the duke himself), a complex cedar maze which provided hours of entertainment for prestigious guests, and it was allegedly built upon the ruins of an ancient monastery.

Some said the complex network of subterranean passages beneath the palace was haunted by the monks, but Adelaide did not believe in ghosts. She *did* believe, however, in the properly documented particulars of history, and in that regard, it was a well-known fact that the first Duke of Pembroke had been a close, intimate friend of King Henry VIII, who had awarded the dukedom in the first place.

Yes, indeed. Theodore Sinclair, the current Duke of Pembroke, was the most sought-after bachelor in England, and for some unknown reason, he had taken one look at Adelaide from across a crowded ballroom and fallen head over heels in love with her.

She wasn't sure what she had done to arouse his passions to such a heightened degree. She had danced with him twice at the ball where they met, then accepted his invitations to go walking in the park the following three days in a row, and had sat with him in his box at the theater the following week.

She could not deny her own infatuation, for the duke was very handsome and very grand. Even now she was distracted by the image of his fine muscular form, his charming smile, and the flattery of it all.

And then ... he had come to her father practically *begging* for her hand in marriage. Her father had agreed and was now his old self again, pleased that his family circumstances would improve, as were her sisters who would also benefit from her marriage.

Which was why this letter was probably a mistake.

Adelaide set down her quill.

No ... I must not write to William. It would be the equivalent of sticking a hot poker into a hornet's nest and stirring it around.

She was engaged to Theodore now. William had been gone from Yorkshire for more than a year, and he had left without expressing any feelings for her, other than friendship. She had shed enough tears and waited too long for letters that never came. Her good sense told her she must forget him once and for all and move on with her life. Without him.

Rising hastily from the chair, she padded across her candlelit bedchamber to the fireplace. The flames danced wildly in the grate and the charred log snapped and crackled in the silence of the room.

It was nearly midnight. She should go to sleep and forget about the past. In three weeks she would marry one of the greatest men in England and become Duchess of Pembroke. Her family would rise very high in the world, and she suspected there was some promise of a generous settlement that would end her father's financial hardships.

Knowing that she must act responsibly and dutifully, she padded back to her desk, crumpled the letter that began with 'Dear Mr. Thomas,' and threw it into the fire. Then she snuffed out the candle and climbed into bed.

⌘

The following day, Adelaide struggled with her decision not to write to William.

How can I marry without a word to him? Surely he deserves to know. What will happen when—if—he comes home from Italy and discovers I am a duchess and had not told him a single thing about it? He will be shocked and very hurt.

Adelaide frowned.

Despite the fact that William had inflicted great pain and frustration upon her lately—for he had not written a word since February—she could not bear the idea of hurting him. All her life he had been her closest friend. She could not take this step without telling him. He must hear it from her, and no one else.

That was it, then.

After dinner, she sat down at her desk and brushed the feather quill across her chin. She would write this letter and send it to him in Italy. William probably wouldn't even receive it until after the wedding—so there would be no danger of him talking her out of it—but at least he would know she had cared enough to explain herself to him personally. And though she was angry with him for leaving her behind, she did care, more than words could say. More than she should.

Carefully dipping her quill into the rich black ink, she touched it to the page and began, at last, to write.

My dear Mr. Thomas,
There is something I must tell you ...

Two

WILLIAM WAS HALF IN his cups when he returned home from the doctor's dinner party at the villa. He had not yet learned how to keep pace with the Italians and their constant flow of fine wine, but he was no quitter, dammit. And by God, he enjoyed their hospitality and was learning a great deal about things that were of enormous interest to him.

Human anatomy. Medicines. The workings of the brain.

They were fascinating subjects, and he was thankful to have been given the opportunity to travel here. Though he had not expected to remain so long.

Two years ago his sister had married an Italian count. Nine months later, William had come, at his father's request, to acquaint himself with his new nephew.

Little did William know that he would discover a new passion, a life's calling, while in the presence of his hosts. It happened on the day he arrived, when they'd introduced him to their neighbor, Giulio Donatello, a prominent Italian physician and medical researcher.

Since that day, William had immersed himself in every medical book he could lay his hands on, and was considering a life devoted to science and discovery and medicine, despite the fact that his father would most certainly frown on such pursuits. His father considered any profession outside of the church or the army to be well beneath his sons, for they were aristocrats—though not very highborn aristocrats in the greater scheme of things. William's father was viscount, and as a second son, William was a mere 'mister.'

Not that it mattered. William never coveted his father's title. Instead, he craved freedom—freedom to choose his own path in life.

And tonight he felt positively euphoric. Donatello had invited him to attend a dinner at the Vatican the following week with a group of physicians that had come all the way from Amsterdam.

As William made his way up the stairs to his bedchamber, he realized it had been months since he'd written a letter home. He felt a sudden compulsion to pick up his quill and write to Adelaide about all that had happened recently. He wished she were here so that he could show her all the wonders of Rome. It had been too long since they'd sat in the same room together, or went riding across the moors, or swam under the waterfall on her father's estate. God, how he missed her.

She would celebrate her nineteenth birthday soon. A woman, at last. Perhaps, finally, it was time to go home, for he had been waiting a very long time to declare his feelings. His whole life, it seemed.

When he reached the door to his bedchamber, he entered quietly, as it was late and he did not wish to wake anyone in the household.

He closed the door behind him and set the candle down on the cabinet to his left.

Shrugging out of his dinner jacket, he glanced at the fireplace. The kindling was laid out for him, but he did not wish to light a fire on such a warm summer night. A few candles at his desk would serve him well enough.

William tossed his jacket over the upholstered bench at the foot of his bed, but as he tugged at his neck cloth, he noticed a letter on the corner of the desk. It must have been delivered while he was out.

Quickly, he crossed to it, picked it up, and turned it over. As he beheld the familiar red seal, his heart leapt, for the letter had come from Adelaide. What perfect timing.

Surely there was some form of destiny at play here, for now that he knew his true purpose in the world, he had been thinking such wonderful thoughts about the sort of future they could enjoy together.

He tore eagerly at the seal, sat down in the chair, and began to read ...

> My dear Mr. Thomas,
> There is something I must tell you. It hardly seems possible that I am writing this. I cannot believe it has been almost two years since you left Yorkshire. I am sorry for not writing to you more often these past few months, but recently I have been rather swept away by circumstances that I must now convey to you.
> In May, I visited London for part of the Season. At one particular ball, I was introduced to a most illustrious person, His Grace, the Duke of Pembroke. If you

were here, I would tell you every detail, but I cannot possibly write the words. To put it plainly, the duke has asked for my hand in marriage, and I have accepted. His Grace does not desire a lavish or extravagant wedding, so we will be married at his private family chapel, at Pembroke, in July.

The whole world turned white before William's eyes. He rose abruptly from his chair and knocked it over onto the floor.

Adelaide had accepted a marriage proposal from a duke? No, it could not be!

I wonder what you must be thinking as you read these words. I hope you are not too terribly astonished.

This feels strange. I wish you had been here to advise me before I made my choice of a husband. You have always been my closest, dearest friend, and you have always told me the truth, even if it was not what I wanted to hear. But in this case, I am sure you would approve.

The duke is a handsome, pleasant, and very wealthy man. I am sure I do not need to explain what this means for my family. Father has been doting over me like never before, treating me like a fragile piece of porcelain, indulging my every whim. I am happy, of course, that he is so pleased, but there is a part of me that is unsure.

I wish you were not so far away, for you would know just how to ease my mind. You would help me remember my duty.

Perhaps I shouldn't be writing to you like this, but I could not take this step without some word to you. I felt you must hear it from me.

Please know that you will remain my dearest friend, William, and I will never forget what we were to each other, growing up as we did as neighbors here on the moors of Yorkshire.

Wish me well, as I will wish you well in return.

The next time you see me, I will be a duchess, but I promise to always remain the girl you knew.

— Adelaide

His stomach in knots, William slowly bent forward and picked up the chair so that he could sink down onto it. He sat for a long moment, stunned, trembling in the heart, then tossed the letter onto the desk as if it were infected with the plague.

A sickening ball of confusion rolled over in his gut while he fought to comprehend the truth of what he had just read. Perhaps this was not real. Perhaps she was playing a trick on him.

But no ... Adelaide would never toy with his emotions in such a manner. They were friends. *More* than friends. They had always understood each other intimately, as few people do.

He had imagined she would wait for him, that when he came home to Yorkshire, he would propose marriage and she would accept. Had he not been clear about that? Had she not recognized his feelings and understood that she was far more than a friend to him? Apparently not.

It killed him to know that her father had taken Adelaide to London for the Season. In a way, William had considered her to be his own discovery, perhaps even his own private possession. They lived in the remote northern country. There had never been any competition from other men for her affections. Her father had no money to spare, so even the thought of a London Season for Adelaide had seemed out of reach.

William should have known better. He should not have taken her for granted. He should have predicted that her father would find a way to present her to important people.

William buried his face in his hands. It had been a mistake to remain in Italy so long and presume she would not venture out into the world without him. What a fool he had been to assume she would remain his.

But what was he to do now? Was it too late? Had he lost her forever?

No, that was not possible. She was *his*, and no other man would ever understand her, worship her, *love* her as he did.

Suddenly he was dragging his trunk out of the dressing room and tossing clothes into it with a mad urgency he could barely fathom.

He penned a brief note to Donatello to apologize for his unexpected departure, and to send his regrets regarding the upcoming dinner at the Vatican.

'A personal emergency,' William called it.

Indeed it was an emergency. Would he reach England in time? Or would he arrive too late to pour out his heart in plain words, as he should have done before, and stop one of the most prestigious weddings of the decade?

Three

Pembroke Palace
Two days before the wedding ...

*T*WIRLING THEIR PARASOLS OVER their heads, Adelaide and her two sisters, Mary and Margarite, strolled leisurely along the white gravel path in the Italian Gardens. The air was thick and humid, and Adelaide felt uncomfortably warm beneath the relentless rays of the sun.

She paused at the stone fountain and gazed up at the statue of Venus in the center. "Upon my word, the heat is stifling. I wish we could kick off our shoes and splash around in the water. Do you think Venus would mind?"

Margarite raised an eyebrow. "No, she would probably enjoy the entertainment, but Father would brain us if he caught us behaving like uncivilized country bumpkins. It's hardly the impression he wishes to convey, now that we are here at Pembroke."

"Mm," Adelaide replied thoughtfully. "In that regard, people have been rather critical about this marriage, have they not? I suspect they are suspicious about why it is happening so quickly. They are probably wondering how someone like me lured the famous Duke of Pembroke into my web and trapped him there."

"Someone like *you?*" Margarite replied. "You are a golden beauty, Adelaide. Everyone sees it but you."

"They are just jealous," Mary assured her. "For years the duke has been an impossible catch. He has showed no interest in matrimony until you came along. It was love at first at sight, and it drives them all mad with envy."

Adelaide sat down on the lichen-covered wall of the fountain and angled her parasol against the blinding sun.

"Do you really believe in love at first sight?" she asked. "The duke barely knows me, nor I him. On the surface he is very handsome and amiable, and he certainly flatters me with his attentions and treats me with the utmost respect. But it is not as I imagined it would be." She paused. "If you must know, I am anxious about the wedding night."

Her sisters exchanged a knowing look, then each sat down on either side of her.

"It's normal to be nervous," Margarite said. "All brides are, but everything will be fine. The duke is an experienced man. He will show you what to do. Do not fret. And it will get easier after the first time."

Adelaide swallowed uneasily. "I am sure you are right, for you are a married woman now, Margarite, and you have far more experience than I."

The back door of the palace swung open just then. A liveried footman appeared, crossed over the flagstone terrace, and strode purposefully down the steps. In a gloved hand, he carried a golden salver.

"He has a letter," Mary said. "I wonder which one of us it is for."

They all stood up and waited. The footman's shiny buckled shoes crunched noisily over the gravel as he approached. Adelaide couldn't help but notice the perspiration dripping from under his white wig.

What a silly ensemble on a day such as this, she thought. Then she wondered if she truly was cut out to be a duchess. How would she ever manage?

The footman arrived and bowed to her. "A letter, my lady."

She glanced down at the gold plate and winced at the blinding reflection of the sun as she picked up the letter. "Thank you."

He bowed again, then turned and began the long trek back to the palace.

"Who is it from?" Mary asked.

Immediately, Adelaide recognized the dark blue seal, and her pulse began to race. The summer heat seemed suddenly intensified, and she was forced to sit down again on the fountain wall.

"It is from Mr. Thomas," she explained as she broke the seal.

Her sisters sat down on either side of her and leaned close to read over her shoulder, but she could not possibly allow that. She rose to her feet and strode off across the green grass to read it alone.

My darling Adelaide,

Forgive me for such intimacies when you are about to be married, but I must speak from my heart. I received your letter about your engagement, and I have come home to declare myself.

You said I was your closest friend, and I remain ever so. Nothing matters more to me than your happiness. For that reason,

I must assure myself that you are certain
of your path, and that you are in full
possession of the facts before you embark
upon a lifelong journey you cannot undo.

Please see me one last time before your
wedding. I am not far from you now. I am
staying at the inn in Pembroke Village, and I
will come to the estate at dusk. I will wait for
you at the entrance to the maze.

— William

Before Adelaide could fully comprehend the
situation, she found herself scanning the horizon, as
if William would suddenly gallop out of the distant
forest, ride toward her, scoop her up onto the back of
his horse and ride away with her.

Her heart raced. He was back! He had returned
from abroad. How she longed to see him!

A hand touched her shoulder, and she jumped.

"What does it say?" Margarite asked with a frown.

Adelaide quickly folded the letter. "It says he has
come home from Italy, and he is here in Pembroke
Village. I can hardly believe it."

"Does he wish to attend your wedding?" Mary
asked innocently. "Good heavens, will the duke allow
it? It is a very small guest list. Family only. I believe he
ordered quail. A very specific number!"

Mary seemed quite concerned about the menu.

Adelaide met Margarite's concerned gaze and
knew at once that her older sister recognized a danger
here, and understood there was far more to this
sticky situation than maintaining a proper headcount
for quail.

"He wants to meet me at the maze," Adelaide
confessed. "At dusk."

"But why?" Mary asked.

With growing unease, Adelaide cleared her throat and tried to maintain her composure. "I am sure you must recall, Mary, that he was always very protective of me. I suppose he wishes to assure himself that I know what I am doing."

"Well, of course you know what you are doing!" Margarite replied incredulously. "You are about to become a duchess, for pity's sake."

Adelaide spoke firmly. "He wants to satisfy himself that I have no reservations about it."

"*Do* you?" Mary asked, sounding completely shocked and bewildered.

Adelaide squared her shoulders and replied too quickly. "Of course I have no reservations, but that is neither here nor there. The point is ..." She paused. "I have not seen William in over a year. You both know he is a dear friend to me. I must go to him, if only to say hello ... and good-bye."

Margarite gripped her arm. The pads of her fingers dug painfully into Adelaide's flesh. "You must not do that. It will confuse you."

"I will not become confused," Adelaide argued. "I know how fortunate I am to be marrying Theodore, and I *will* wed him in two days' time. Nothing is going to change that."

Margarite's grip on her arm tightened. "Are you sure about that? You say William is only a friend, but—"

Adelaide had no intention of allowing her sister to finish that thought. "I am not a fool."

They stared at each other heatedly. "Then why would you even consider going to meet another man—who so clearly has designs upon your affections—mere days before your wedding? If you were truly devoted to the duke, you would not risk your future with him. You would be loyal. Do not go there, Adelaide. You can say good-bye to William in a letter. *After* you are married."

Adelaide tugged her arm free and glanced up at the white palace. It was impossible to imagine not seeing William in person now that he was home. She could not simply leave him waiting at the maze alone, without any explanation.

Margarite's eyes narrowed with suspicion. "What has happened between the two of you? I thought you were friends, nothing more."

"We *are* friends," she insisted. "Nothing has happened."

"Has he ever kissed you?" Margarite asked. "Or touched you?"

It was Mary's turn to grab hold of her other arm. "For that matter, has the *duke* kissed you?"

"That is completely irrelevant!" Margarite scolded Mary. "They are engaged to be married! But if there had been some past affair between Adelaide and Mr. Thomas, it could become complicated. Are you a virgin, Adelaide?"

"Good heavens!" she replied, horrified that her sister would ask such a thing. "Of course I am! And there was no affair." She backed away from them. "William and I are just ..." She paused. "We are very familiar with each other. That is all. He cares for me. Like a brother."

A brother? Oh God. She was going to burn in hell for uttering such a lie, for she had never thought of William as a brother.

Therein lay the problem at the moment. The deception of those words hit her like a wooden club across the chest.

Margarite shook her head with a warning. "Do not make this mistake, Adelaide. Not when we have come so far. The duke will lift us up very high in Society. Think of your future children. They will be heirs to a dukedom and will inherit a great fortune one day." She waved a finger. "Do not, under any circumstances, meet Mr. Thomas at the maze. Be sensible and let him go."

Her advice cut Adelaide to the core, for she knew her sister spoke the truth. She could not meet William two days before her marriage to another man. The words in his letter were clear. After all this time—when she had finally given up on him—he had come home to declare himself.

Part of her hated him for it—for staying away so long. For not giving her some hope before now.

For ever leaving in the first place.

Oh, why did she write that letter? She should have known this would happen.

Perhaps she *had* known.

The idea that she wanted any of this frightened her. She had been so sure of her decision to marry the duke.

Margarite was right. Adelaide could not meet William at dusk. If she did, it could ruin everything.

She must accept that her friendship with William—as she once knew it—was over. She must steel herself against what was, and what might have been, for she was about to become a duchess, and everything was going to change.

Four

WILLIAM GALLOPED FAST AND hard to reach the maze before dusk. He dismounted under an oak tree in a sheltering copse where he could tether his horse out of view of the palace windows.

The heat was stifling, but he barely noticed as he strode along the square-clipped cedars on the outside wall of the maze. When he found the entrance, he quickly slipped inside while struggling to comprehend the complexities of his emotions, and his presence there—a continent away from the world he had come to know so well in the past year. How impulsive he'd been to rush away from all that he found fascinating—science and the study of medicine—to pursue his dream of love. He had been so passionate to stop this wedding. It was as if he would explode like a keg of gunpowder if he did not see Adelaide again and claim her for his own.

Would she come to him tonight? Was this his destiny, and hers? Or had he been a bloody fool to think she might love him that way? Enough to throw aside a wealthy duke and disappoint her father and sisters? Perhaps even be disowned?

Would she take on all that, to marry a mere medical man?

A blackbird fluttered out of the cedars overhead as he continued along the tall green hedges, careful not to venture too deeply into the maze, lest he become lost in the dark and fail to return to meet Adelaide when she arrived.

If she arrived ...

Turning back, he strode to the entrance to sit down and wait.

He would wait all night if he had to, for he could not lose her.

༄༅༷

When William checked his pocketwatch for the hundredth time, his heart was in shreds.

It was past midnight and Adelaide had not come.

With excruciating regret, he rose to his feet, looked up at the stars, and wondered what the bloody hell he was doing here in this dark maze, when clearly Adelaide had made up her mind and he had misunderstood the letter she wrote.

He turned to leave, determined to forget her, determined to bury the past and the foolish hopes he had clung to, but stopped abruptly when his weary eyes locked upon the most exquisite vision ...

There, in the moonlit entrance to the maze, stood Adelaide, her golden hair falling loose and windblown about her shoulders, her chest heaving as if she had run a great distance. He imagined her fleeing from the palace—running recklessly across the wide, rolling green lawns beneath the starlit sky—to reach him.

His darling Adelaide. She was so beautiful, so grown-up since he had last seen her. A woman now. A woman who was soon to become another man's wife.

Anger and hostility coursed through him—along with a barbaric desire to hoist her over his shoulder, toss her onto the back of his horse, and gallop away with her to parts unknown.

Slowly, carefully, he approached. As he drew closer, however, the scorn he saw in her eyes left him pained and disoriented.

"What are you doing here, William?" she asked with a frown. "Why are you doing this?"

Why? God ... Why indeed?

"I had to see you," he explained, but it was a pathetic response, for it did not touch the convoluted condition of his reasoning, his heightened desires, or his selfishness at this moment, because he wanted her at any price. He had claimed in his letter that he would place her happiness above all, but that was a lie. Seeing her now, after so much time apart, he felt a deep arousal in his body and feared that if he did not win her hand, it would be the death of him.

"You had no right to say what you did in your letter," she said as she pulled her shawl tighter around her shoulders. "It's been almost two years since you left Yorkshire, and you haven't written to me in months. Whatever we were to each other then—and I am not even sure *what* we were—it is no longer the case." Her eyes flashed with emotion and her bosom rose and fell as her breathing quickened. She glanced back at the palace, almost desperately. "I shouldn't have come here. Margarite warned me. I don't know why I did."

She turned to leave, but he dashed forward to block her way. "You came because you care for me."

Her gaze lifted to meet his. "Yes, but as a friend. Nothing more."

He shook his head. "I don't believe you. We've always been more than friends, Adelaide. You know it as well as I."

Her eyes raked over his shoulders and chest. He had loosened his neck cloth in the heat, and his shirt was open slightly. She wet her lips. For the first time, a clear, sensuous heat passed between them.

"Then why did you leave without some sort of understanding between us?" she challenged.

"You were too young," he explained.

"I was not so very young. I was old enough to dream of you. To want you. And why did you not come back sooner?"

He let go of her arm and stepped back. "I didn't intend to stay away so long, but I always thought ..."

"You thought what?"

A shadow of despair darkened her eyes, and he was glad. He *wanted* her to feel pain, so that she would not marry the duke.

"I thought that when I came home," he honestly explained, "you would be there waiting for me."

"How arrogant of you." She adjusted her shawl around her shoulders and steeled her posture. "There was no promise between us, William. You did not propose before you left. If you had, I would have waited because God knows I loved you. But you did not. What was I to think? When you stopped writing months ago, I assumed ..." Her chest heaved with a deep intake of breath. "If you must know, I expected you to come home with a bride on your arm—if you ever came home at all—so I forced myself to forget you. And now I have moved on."

"No," he replied with a frown. "You're lying. Otherwise you would not have written me that letter, and you certainly would not be here now, alone with me at midnight."

She bristled at that. "I am here to say good-bye to you because I consider you a friend," she explained, "and I felt you deserve to know the truth."

"And what is the truth exactly?" he asked, taking hold of her arm again. "In your letter you said you were unsure, and I know you too well to believe that anything has changed. I see it in your eyes, Adelaide. You have doubts. Admit it."

She tried again to leave but he would not release her.

"I am not admitting anything to you," she said.

"Not to *me*," he replied. "To yourself. Do you love him?"

Adelaide stared at him irately, then wheeled around and ventured deeper into the maze, as if she could escape him—and the question. But there was no hope of that. He would not give up. He would *never* give up.

"Do you love him?" he repeated, more forcefully as she veered left into another cedar-lined corridor, her skirts whipping about her legs as she strode fast beneath the silvery moon.

Suddenly she stopped, stood still for a moment, and finally turned around. "Step aside, William," she said. "We are going to get lost in here, and I must go back."

"Answer me first," he said. "If you tell me you truly love Pembroke with all your heart, I swear I will leave you now and never mention any of this again. I will return to Italy, knowing that you are happy."

She was breathing heavily now. Her brow was furrowed. "He is very devoted to me," she explained. "He has been a gentleman in every way, and he is a duke. The Duke of Pembroke! Have you any idea what this means to my family?"

William hesitated, then spoke in a quiet, calmer voice. "Still, you have not answered the question ... And yet you have."

The crickets chirped noisily in the grass outside the maze, and a gentle breeze whispered over the evergreen hedges.

"I respect him," Adelaide said at last. "He is intelligent, witty, and very attentive. Might I also add that he is handsome? I will not deny that I was infatuated when he first asked me to dance and when he invited me to go walking in the park. I had butterflies in my belly when his coach arrived to escort us to the theater. It was all very exciting, William. Very flattering."

Upon listening to this, William wanted to retch up the contents of his stomach.

Then he wanted to march through the palace gates, storm into the house, and choke the Duke of Pembroke until he turned blue.

Adelaide continued. "When he proposed, I felt ..."

"Yes?"

"Triumphant. I still feel that way."

William fought to control the feral jealousy that was burning a hole in his gut. He balled his hands into fists, stared long and hard into Adelaide's eyes, and fought to see into her soul as he always could—for she had never held anything back from him.

Tonight, however, her eyes were cool and steely. Guarded. It was as if she had slammed a door in his face.

Clearly she was angry with him for leaving, and had made every effort to banish him from her heart. She was struggling to do so now.

Adelaide raised her chin as if to communicate, in no uncertain terms, that she would not be deterred.

Perhaps he was wrong to have come here. Perhaps she *had* changed from the free-spirited young girl he once knew. Or perhaps she had hidden that person away, buried her forever in the depths of her duty and ambition.

William's eyebrows pulled together with dismay. Grief poured through him. Had he truly lost her? Was this the end?

"Then you are sure?" he asked, taking a step back, fighting to understand.

"Yes, I think so," she firmly replied.

Something sparked and flared in his heart. "You *think* so," he said. "That is not convincing enough, Adelaide. Not for me."

She inclined her head at him, in that way she always did, to warn him against pushing her too hard.

"Do not dissect my every word, William. You must simply accept that I have made my decision, and I do not wish to alter it."

For a long excruciating moment they stared at each other in the moonlight, while the night breeze continued to blow through the hedges. William felt as if the walls of cedar were closing in on him. He wanted to grab hold of Adelaide, shake her, then pull her into his arms and hold her—so tight that she could not escape him, not until she realized she was making a dreadful mistake. That she was *his*. That she could not marry another, not even a duke.

"Please, William ... you must say good-bye to me now," she whispered. "Let us part as friends." She held out her hand.

No. This was wrong. He would not shake her hand. He would not say good-bye. His mind wandered to other times. Good times they'd shared.

"Before we bid each other farewell," he said, "and before you become a duchess, permit me to make a request."

"Yes?"

"Meet me again tomorrow, as we used to do in Yorkshire. Remember?"

Her eyes clouded over with apprehension. "We are not children anymore, William. I cannot go running with you across the moors, or fishing at dawn, or swimming in the rain. I am about to become a married woman."

"But you are not married yet." He spoke lightly, his tone persuasively friendly and open. "Come and meet me. We will talk and laugh. I want to know everything I have missed since I left Yorkshire. Is Mrs. Jenkins' goat still roaming in Mrs. Smith's vegetable garden?"

Adelaide hesitated, then her shoulders relaxed slightly. "Yes, but it's much worse now, for Mrs. Jenkins has three new goats who like to follow their leader."

William smiled, for there it was—a hint of the girl he once knew. She had not disappeared after all, at least not yet.

"Will you see me tomorrow?" he pressed. "I saw a charming lake house on my way here, and there is a walking path around the lake. Could you sneak away for a short while?"

She thought about it, and glanced over her shoulder. "I do not like that word ... *sneak*."

"Call it whatever you wish. I will be at the lake house all day," he said, "and I will wait for you there." *As long as I have to.*

And somehow I will change your mind.

Then suddenly, unexpectedly, her expression softened and to his utter shock and delight, she stepped into his arms and hugged him.

He was so taken aback, all the air rushed from his lungs, and it took a moment for him to gather his wits about him.

When at last he could breathe again, he cupped the back of her head with his hand and buried his face against her neck.

Desire flowed through him as he breathed in the sweet scent of her skin and felt the soft silk of her hair upon his cheeks. He was so overwhelmed by her touch that the ground shifted beneath him, and he regretted ever leaving Yorkshire. Regretted it terribly, for he knew this was the end.

She was saying good-bye.

Quickly, she stepped back before he could do anything to prevent it. "I must go before someone discovers I am missing and sends out the dogs."

She might as well have reached into his chest and ripped his heart out.

"We cannot have that," he gallantly replied, while he fought to control his agony. He was not ready to give up. There had to be a way to stop this tragedy from playing out.

When they reached the maze entrance, he took hold of her hand, raised it to his lips, and laid a soft kiss upon her knuckles. His heart pounded feverishly, and when he spoke, his voice shook.

"I will always love you, Adelaide."

As she withdrew her hand from his grasp, all joy left his body.

Then he felt her palm upon his cheek. It was soft and gentle in the night.

Slowly, his eyes lifted. He laid his hand on top of hers and gazed at her with heated lust, which was wildly improper and indiscreet, but he could hide nothing from this woman.

Her eyes glistened with wetness, and a tear fell across her cheek.

Ah, Adelaide . . .

Turning his lips into her palm, he kissed it firmly, lingeringly. When she offered no resistance, he kissed her slender wrist, then traveled up the soft flesh of her inner arm until he reached the inside crook of her elbow.

She sucked in a breath of shock, but it was mixed with desire.

A wild sense of satisfaction filled him. Unable to control his lust for her, he took her face in his hands and claimed her sweet, succulent mouth with his own.

Her lips parted for him. They were moist and hot beneath the ravenous heat of his kiss. While his tongue mingled with hers, his hands traveled down her neck and across her shoulders until he slid the silken shawl away. It fluttered lightly to the ground. Adelaide moaned with pleasure as she rose up on her toes to wrap her arms around his neck.

The increased pace of her breathing and the intoxicating evidence of her pleasure sent a firestorm of arousal into William's core, and he pulled her tighter against him.

She trembled and went weak in his arms, and surrendered at last to what had always existed between them but had never been explored.

"Oh William," she sighed as she threw her head back in rapture.

His blood coursed hotly through his veins. As he dragged his voracious mouth to the front of her throat, he moaned and blazed a trail of hot kisses down to her collarbone. His tongue darted out to savor the sweet essence of her skin.

"You're mine, Adelaide," he whispered, his voice husky and low. He drew back and took her face in his hands. "Follow your heart and come away with me. We will go to Italy together. I will marry you and love you forever."

Bewildered and shaking, she wet her lips and clung to his jacket collar as if pleading with him. "Why didn't you say all of this before? Why did you wait so long, when now it is too late?"

He touched his forehead to hers and shut his eyes. "It is not too late."

"Yes, it is. I do love you, William. I always have, but I just don't know ..."

His eyes flew open. "Yes, you *do* know. You must think of your own happiness. There is more to life than duty. Let us go now," he pressed.

"No, I cannot. I must think first ..."

"Then meet me tomorrow," he said.

When she continued to hesitate, he pulled the ruby ring from his finger, placed it into her open palm, and closed her fingers over it. "This is my promise to you, before God. I *will* be your husband, Adelaide, if only you will come to me."

Holding the ring in a tight fist, she pressed it to her heart.

"Yes," she said at last, and the whole world turned bright before his eyes. "Wait for me tomorrow at the lake house." She began to back away from him. "I will come to you after dark."

He stepped forward to follow, desperate not to lose her. "Do you promise?"

"Yes. I swear it. Nothing will keep me from you." Then she turned to go, waving one last time before she broke into a run.

And just like that, joy flooded back into his body, and his heart exploded into a thousand stars as he dropped to his knees in relief.

Five

SHORTLY AFTER SUNSET THE following day, Adelaide gathered her hat in her hands, placed it on her head, and tied the ribbon under her chin. She crossed her bedchamber and opened the door, but sucked in a breath of shock when she found her father leaning against the opposite wall in the corridor, arms folded over his chest, nostrils flaring as he gazed at her.

"Where do you think you're going?" he asked accusingly as he pushed away from the wall and crowded her back into her bedchamber.

"It's a lovely evening for a walk," she calmly explained.

He entered the room and shut the door behind him. He was a tall man and he towered over her like a giant. "Do not lie to me, Adelaide. I know where you were last night. I know you went to the maze at midnight to meet Mr. Thomas. Margarite told me everything."

Adelaide frowned. How had Margarite known? Adelaide had assured her sister that she would not go to meet William. At the time, she had believed in her own heart that she could, and would, resist seeing him again. But in the end she had left her room with the utmost urgency and gone dashing across the moonlit gardens to reach him.

Margarite must have expected her to change her mind. She may even have spied on her.

"I did nothing wrong," she told her father. "Mr. Thomas is a friend. I felt I owed him an explanation."

"Why?"

"Because he ..." She paused, then raised her chin, squared her shoulders, and spoke with a purposeful degree of condescension. "Because as you must know, he fancies himself in love with me. I had to set him straight, and make sure he understood that I had made up my mind, and we could never be together."

Her father's eyes narrowed until he was squinting at her. "Then where are you going tonight?"

"Nowhere," she replied too quickly. "A walk. There is no cause for alarm. I was firm with Mr. Thomas, and he is gone now. I suspect he is already halfway to Italy."

Her heart was pounding violently in her chest and she prayed her father could not recognize her panic.

For a long moment he studied her expression. Then his eyes softened and he moved closer. He took her shoulders in his hands and spoke compassionately, as if she were still a child and she had just lost her puppy.

"I know how it is between you and Mr. Thomas," he gently said. "There is a bond there, for you grew up together, but I cannot let you make this mistake, Adelaide. It is only because he has been away for so long that you romanticize what you were to each other."

She shook her head and argued, "I am not romanticizing—"

He raised a finger to his lips. "Shh. You must listen to reason. Look around you. You have made it all the way to Pembroke Palace. It is your destiny to become duchess here. The duke adores you. He would have paid any sum to have you. You must let go of the past and walk down the aisle tomorrow to marry the man who is meant to be your husband. Surely you feel it. Surely you understand that Mr. Thomas is merely a distraction."

Adelaide swallowed painfully over a lump in her throat. "Of course I know that," she replied. "I am not a fool, Father."

"Good." He dropped his hands to his sides and headed for the door. "But just to be sure ..." He paused at the threshold. "I am going to lock you in."

Adelaide's eyes widened with shock. A burning mix of rage and terror flared through her body as she lunged forward to stop him.

The door slammed shut before she could reach it. The key turned in the lock.

"Father, no!" She pounded hard against it.

"It is for your own protection," he said from the other side. "You will thank me later. You'll see."

"No, I will not! I will never thank you! You mustn't do this!" She wrestled with the latch and kicked the door repeatedly.

"I will tell the duke that you are unwell this evening," her father said, "and that you must rest. If you shout or continue to act like a spoiled child, Adelaide, I will come in there and beat you senseless. Do you understand?"

Adelaide felt suddenly light-headed, for she knew her father well. He did not make idle threats, and he had beaten her once before. Only once, however, for she had learned her lesson the first time and had never defied him again.

Or rather, she had never been *caught* defying him.

Slowly she backed away from the door while her heart pounded like a hammer. *Please God ... This cannot be happening.*

She turned and rushed to the window to look outside. The sun had set in splashes of pink and orange on the distant horizon. Soon it would be dark and William would expect her at the lake house.

How long would he wait?

What if she could not escape and he believed she had changed her mind?

She opened the window and leaned out. Was it possible to jump or climb to freedom?

No. She was too high up and would surely die in the attempt.

Adelaide shut the window again. Her gaze darted about the room desperately to seek some means of escape. Her father had said it was her destiny to marry the duke, but she could not believe it.

She loved William. She would *always* love William, and she knew in the deepest realms of her soul that it was her destiny to grow old with him. But how ... how would she ever reach him?

ᘒᘓᘒ

Perhaps it was not her destiny after all, Adelaide thought miserably as she slipped into bed at nearly two in the morning.

She had tried everything. She had pulled the velvet rope and rang for her maid, pleaded every excuse she could think of to get out of her room, but her father was always there, sitting outside her bedchamber, watching her with hooded eyes, listening to every word she spoke.

Eventually she had done exactly what he warned her against. She had screamed and pounded on the door and cried for help, and her father had proven true to his word. He walked in, shut the door behind him, and slapped her hard across the face. He threatened worse if she did not keep quiet.

Then he said something that made her blood run cold. He promised to direct his wrath and violence toward William if she did not do her duty and walk down the aisle as planned.

It was now three o'clock in the morning, and her wedding would take place that very day, in eight hours' time.

Her heart had broken to pieces.

Had William given up on her yet? Did he believe she had changed her mind, or would he gallop through the chapel doors on his great black steed in the morning, like a courageous medieval knight, and spirit her away before the vicar could begin the ceremony?

Oh, now she was just being foolish, dreaming of fairy tales and what could never be ...

Adelaide squeezed her eyes shut.

William ... if you can hear me across the distance, know that I love you and I tried to reach you. I will never forget the magic of our kiss in the moonlight ...

Then a cool breeze wafted across the bed and fluttered her hair. There was a creaking sound, like a door opening and closing.

Adelaide sat up in the darkness and glanced at the door, but it was still locked.

A sudden panic filled her, for she had heard the stories about the spirit monks who haunted the subterranean passages of this palace. She had never believed in ghosts before, but a keen awareness tingled down her spine—a sense of something about to happen.

Then a hand covered her mouth and her heart leapt into her throat. Once she calmed, the hand loosened and she knew in her heart who had come for her ...

"William?"

Was she dreaming? Was he truly there, standing beside her bed, or was it some spirit from beyond?

He was cloaked in shadow, but somehow she knew he was real. She could feel him in her soul.

"You must be very quiet," he whispered as he sat down on the edge of the bed.

She nodded in agreement, her spine ramrod straight.

He took his hand away from her mouth and cupped her cheek. "Are you all right?"

"Yes," she whispered. "I wanted to come to you. I tried."

"I know."

"Father locked me in."

"I suspected as much."

She felt her forehead wrinkle in confusion. "But how did you get in here? Did you come through the window?"

He shook his head. "I have not yet learned to fly, darling. When you did not come, I ran as fast as I could to the palace, to the servants' entrance, and tried to sneak in."

"What happened?"

"The housekeeper took me for a thief and tossed me out on my backside. I had almost given up and was about to return to the village when a footman approached me. He told me about the secret passages and offered to take me to your chamber—for a price."

"That was very unscrupulous of him," she said.

"I agree, but I paid him nonetheless. He had just been let go, so I suppose he had an axe to grind." William glanced toward the large tapestry beside the bed. "Did you know there was a door in the wall?"

"No. If I had, I would have used it to sneak out of here hours ago."

Overcome by curiosity, Adelaide slid off the bed and went to examine it. Indeed, there was a secret door behind the tapestry. It opened soundlessly this time to reveal a dark passageway that led somewhere mysterious.

"We can sneak out together," William whispered, "if you are sure this is what you want. My horse is waiting at the stables. If we ride all night, we can make it to London by late tomorrow and board a ship. I will take you to Italy, my love, and I promise you will be very happy there. I have so much to tell you about the discoveries I have made and what I have learned there, what we can do there together—but not now, Adelaide. If we are going to leave before your wedding, we must go."

She nodded, but hesitated and looked around. "Should I bring anything?"

She glanced at the locked door and felt a sudden pang of remorse. Would she ever see her sisters again?

"Your cloak," he replied, "for it has become cool outside, and whatever else you can fit in a small bag."

She hurried across the room, fetched a few things from the wardrobe, and stuffed them into a valise. Then she wrapped her cloak around her shoulders.

William approached and fastened the clasp at her neck.

Their eyes met, and she felt a thrilling wave of excitement for the future, but it was mixed with fear and uncertainty.

"Are you sure about this?" he asked, his expression serious.

"Of course I am. You are everything to me, William. You always were, for as long as I can remember. And knowing you feel as I do, I cannot imagine my life without you."

"Nor can I imagine my life without *you*. I love you, Adelaide. Nothing will ever change that."

Stirred by the power of his love for her, she lifted her face to meet his kiss, which held a promise that would never be broken. She felt it in her heart and in her body—especially when his silken tongue met hers with raw, heated passion. Happiness settled into her, and she knew that William Thomas was the great love of her life.

He kissed her devotedly, then drew back and smiled down at her. "Now it begins," he whispered, as he took her hand and led her across the room to the door behind the tapestry.

"What begins?" she asked.

"Our future together."

Quietly they slipped into the secret, narrow corridor that would see them out of the palace.

Adelaide clasped William's hand tightly as he led her down the dark passageway. Her heart pounded with a combination of fear and daring exhilaration. She felt as if they were prisoners making a brave escape from a dungeon.

They were not out of the woods yet, however. Anything could happen before they reached the stables.

Nevertheless, as they made their way toward freedom, Adelaide knew that nothing would keep them apart. Even if her father caught them, even if he beat her and locked her up again, she and William would find a way to be together somehow, for it was their destiny. He was the other half of her soul.

She had known it the moment he kissed her.

Part Two

Seduced
at
Sunset

Chapter One

*I*N EVERY LIFE, THERE comes a time when one must let go of certain regrets, stop mourning for the paths not taken, and forge ahead into the future with fresh new goals, and somewhat altered expectations.

Standing at the window, looking out over the vast expanse of green lawns and thick forests reaching all the way to the horizon, Lady Charlotte Sinclair raised her teacup to her lips and settled her gaze on the red brick dower house in the distance.

"Do you ever wonder if she's lonely?" Charlotte asked her sister-in-law, Lady Anne, who rose from her chair and came to join her at the window.

"Are you referring to Adelaide?" Anne replied. "She certainly hasn't seemed melancholy, not that I can see. It's been two years now, since the duke passed. I think she is doing remarkably well under the circumstances. Why? Do you feel differently?"

Charlotte set her teacup down upon the saucer with a delicate clink. "I cannot help but wonder if Mother ever thinks about Dr. Thomas. They haven't seen each other since Father's funeral." She turned her eyes to Anne. "You know the story, don't you?

That she attempted to run off with him and flee the palace through the underground tunnels on the eve of her wedding?"

"No, I didn't know that particular detail," Anne said with surprise, looking sharply out the window toward the dower house. "I knew, of course, that she and Dr. Thomas were close at one time, and that they had been sweethearts before she married the duke."

Anne spoke tactfully, well aware that the two were more than sweethearts, for Adelaide had also left her husband for a brief interval during their marriage, and had spent time away from Pembroke with Dr. Thomas. As a result, Charlotte and her twin brother Garrett were born nine months later—one of the many secret scandals hidden within the palace walls.

For years, the secret had been kept safe. No one outside the family knew that Charlotte and Garrett were illegitimate, and that Dr. William Thomas was their true father.

"What in the world happened?" Anne asked. "Because obviously, she didn't jilt the duke at the altar. She went ahead with it. Otherwise she would never have become Duchess of Pembroke."

Charlotte turned to sit on the wide painted windowsill, and set her teacup and saucer down beside her. "Mother told me everything about it shortly before Father passed away. She said she had no regrets about marrying him—that it was her destiny to be duchess here, and mother to all of us, just as we are. Though she loved Dr. Thomas quite passionately in her youth, I believe, in the end, she was content with the choice she had made."

"Naturally I am pleased to hear that," Anne said as she sat down beside Charlotte on the windowsill. "But you still haven't told me what happened on the eve of the wedding. Did she keep the duke waiting at the chapel?"

"No, she was there on time. Her father caught Mother and Dr. Thomas as they were attempting to flee the palace. There was some violence, I believe, and poor Dr. Thomas was dragged away, unconscious. I don't know all the particulars, but Mother chose to walk down the aisle the next day to save him from any further harm. She wrote to him and told him that she had changed her mind, that her father was right, and it was her duty to marry the duke, and that William must never contact her again. When he found out she had gone through with it, he left England and didn't return for a few years. It was when he came back that he and mother spent those ... intimate hours together." Charlotte picked up her tea again. "Father knew nothing about her infidelity until much later, when he realized Garrett and I looked nothing like him or our brothers."

Anne laid a hand over her chest. "Good heavens. That is quite a story," she said.

"Yes, indeed, and I have not been able to push it from my mind since I learned of it. Imagine, poor Dr. Thomas being thumped on the head and dragged out of the tunnels. And poor Mother, who was desperately in love with him ... How she must have suffered. It is quite a tale of woe, which is why I believe it's high time someone made it right. Their day has come, Anne. Do you not agree? Mother was a dutiful wife to the very end, but she is a widow now. And Dr. Thomas—so skilled in the art of medicine—was such a good friend to her when Father was ill. He was her knight in shining armor. Surely they both deserve happiness. They have waited so long."

Anne considered it. "Do you not think they are old enough, and wise enough, to make their own decisions? If they want to be together, there is nothing standing in their way. They can do so without someone—and that would be *you*, I presume—making it happen."

Charlotte smiled. "Of course it would be me. Why do you think I brought it up?" She rose to her feet and went to pour herself another cup of tea. "Dr. Thomas is always delighted to see me when I visit my publisher in London," she said as she picked up the teapot. "I am sure he would be open to an invitation of some sort. Perhaps he just needs a little prodding."

"So you intend to try your hand at matchmaking?" Anne said, intrigued.

"I most certainly do," Charlotte replied. "I am the perfect candidate for such an undertaking. They are my parents, after all, and I know them better than anyone. Besides, I need to have *some* form of romance in my life, even if it is not my own."

Anne and Charlotte had been sisters-in-law for twelve years now. They were the best of friends, and for that reason Charlotte did not need to explain why she had long given up dreaming of her own happily ever after. Charlotte was no stranger to heartache and disappointment, which was probably why she and Dr. Thomas rubbed along so well. She felt a deep connection to him, for he had lost his beloved tragically at an early age, just as she had.

Before that loss, Charlotte had actually believed she was leading a charmed life, for she had met the perfect man during her first week of her first Season in London. Lord Graham Spencer was the most handsome gentleman she had ever seen, with jet-black hair, piercing blue eyes, and a tall muscular build. If his looks weren't enough to make a young lady swoon, he was also charming, intelligent, and exceptionally honorable. To top it all off, he was heir to a dukedom, and was soon to inherit his ailing father's title and estate in Devonshire.

They had fallen in love instantly upon introduction, and the courtship was as passionate and romantic as any woman could ever dream. By the end of the Season Graham had proposed and given Charlotte his grandmother's gigantic diamond ring, and they fell more deeply in love with each passing day as they anticipated their wedding the following spring.

It was a passionate love, and they had both been far too impatient ...

Then, three weeks before Charlotte's highly anticipated walk down the aisle, Graham was thrown from his horse in the middle of London's Trafalgar Square on a sunny afternoon. The coroner told them he died instantly from a head injury, and Charlotte was left to endure the unbearable agony of losing the man she loved with all her heart, and with that, the happy future of which she had dreamed.

A month later, she discovered she was with child. While most women would have feared and dreaded the scandal, Charlotte had wept tears of joy. She announced it to her family with pride—and a careless disregard for how Society would judge her—for in her womb, she carried a piece of her beloved that would stay with her forever.

But fate was cruel to her yet again. At the end of her first trimester, she lost the baby and fell into a deep pit of despair that lasted nearly a year. The grief was immeasurable, and it was a long hard climb back to a life that included any thoughts of the future, for she couldn't possibly imagine how to find happiness again.

And so, she passed through her best years in a quiet state of melancholy. Her family tried to coax her to begin again at the next London Season, or the Season after that, but she had no interest in flirting, and surely no man could possibly compare to Graham, the great love of her life, who had been so cruelly ripped from her world.

Now she was long past a marriageable age, but had found a different sort of happiness from within, and through her writing. A year ago, her first novel *The Boxer* had been published under the pseudonym Victor Edwards, and it was now a literary sensation, which proved to be exceedingly lucrative for Charlotte. The book was in its seventeenth printing and was selling well in Europe as well as America. She had already been commissioned to write a second novel, which was due on her editor's desk next summer.

Hence, her life—though it was not what she imagined it would be when she was young and full of romantic dreams—had turned out to be surprisingly satisfactory.

Nevertheless, Charlotte had recently begun to desire something more ...

She was not a block of ice. She had known passion and desire once before. Though she did not yearn for a life of matrimony—she was financially independent and quite happy in her solitude—her *body* longed for certain physical pleasures with a man. She wanted to be touched, and aroused. *By a lover.* By someone sinfully handsome and experienced. Someone compelling.

She would never be as young as she once was, but by God, she had not lost her looks yet. If she were honest about it, without conceit, she was in fact quite comely, with golden hair and a curvaceous figure. In the right situation, she was confident she could do what was required to attract a desirable candidate for the sort of encounter she had in mind.

"So how do you plan to begin?" Anne asked as she rose from her seat on the windowsill to return to the sofa. "Will you invite Dr. Thomas to Pembroke?"

Charlotte shook away the other fantasy that had been on her mind so often lately and sat down beside Anne. She chose a raspberry scone from the biscuit plate. "Eventually, yes, but first I will pay him a call in London. He is always pleased to see me, as I am his only daughter. Since the Season is in full swing, I shall persuade Mother to accompany me this time. I will suggest that we take in the theater and accept a few invitations to dinners and balls. For years she has been trying to convince me to enjoy myself, so I will inform her that I am ready to do just that."

"Oh, Charlotte." Anne laid a hand on her knee. "Please tell me that you are indeed ready to enjoy yourself, and that it is not simply a charade to lure Adelaide to London."

Charlotte popped the last bite of the scone into her mouth. "I believe I am more than ready," she replied. "I have been too bookish of late. It's time to live a little; do you not agree? Heaven forbid I become a recluse in my old age."

The maid entered to collect the tea tray, and Anne smiled with encouragement. "Will you write to me?" she asked. "And tell me everything?"

"I will write to you each day," Charlotte replied.

Though she was not certain she would be able to divulge *all* the details—for some of the activities she planned to engage in might turn out to be exceedingly private.

Chapter Two

London

*I*MMEDIATELY FOLLOWING THE MEETING with her publisher, Charlotte instructed her coachman to take her to Dr. Thomas's medical offices on Park Lane. A short while later she was greeted by the clerk at the front desk and shown into her father's study, which was located down a narrow red-carpeted corridor at the rear of the clinic.

As always, Charlotte paused at the door to behold the cluttered yet cozy state of the room, with books and papers piled high and spread everywhere, and a faded coat of dark green paint on the walls. Aside from the fact that there was a skeleton standing by the window, the room was quite inviting, though definitely in need of a woman's touch. Dr. Thomas needed some help with organization. Charlotte suspected, however, that too much of it might upset his professional balance. He was a brilliant surgeon who specialized in diseases of the brain, and he probably knew the exact location of every book and document in the building.

This was obviously his sanctuary, his place of private reflection, where he researched the newest methods of scientific investigation. Charlotte was exceedingly proud of her father, and pleased that he derived so much pleasure from his work. He'd told her his work gave his life meaning, even when he had been forced to endure certain disappointments.

He was referring, of course, to the loss of his great love—Charlotte's mother Adelaide, now the Dowager Duchess of Pembroke. It had been years since Charlotte and Dr. Thomas spoke of it, but she knew the hole in his heart would remain there forever, just as the hole in her own heart would always be a part of her. 'Like father like daughter,' he once said to her. 'We are two peas in a pod.'

Not exactly, however, for his lost love was still alive and now attainable. There was hope for them yet.

She heard her father leave one of the examination rooms and approach her from behind. "William," Charlotte said with a warm smile as she waited in the doorway.

They were on intimate enough terms to use their given names, at least in private, but he refused to let her call him 'Papa.' It was not to be acknowledged.

"My darling girl," he said, giving her a quick kiss on the cheek. "What brings you to London? Another meeting with your publisher, I suspect? They must be so pleased with the success of your book."

"Yes, and they are eager for me to finish the next one. My editor had all sorts of questions about it this morning."

"What sorts of questions?" he asked as he moved into the room and closed the door behind them.

Charlotte took a seat in the leather chair in front of the desk and told him more about her meeting.

After they had caught up on each other's news, Charlotte sat forward on the edge of her chair and folded her hands primly on top of her reticule. "Did

I mention that Mother is here in London as well?" she asked. "We intend to stay for what's left of the Season and will probably attend the theater this week. Thursday, perhaps. Tomorrow we will walk in the park. What plans do you have this week, William? Anything of note?"

She spoke in a light, casual tone, so as not to ram too forcefully through the gate in the first five minutes, for she firmly believed that matchmaking required a certain ... *subtlety.* The persons involved in the potential match must not feel they are being pressured, persuaded, or manipulated. They must each believe they, alone, are the source of the attraction, and that they are making their own choices without any outside influences. Each must believe they are holding the reins.

Dr. Thomas sat back in his chair, removed his spectacles, and laid them on the desk. "My plans for the week," he replied, "involve a great deal of research and reading. Which is exciting enough for a man like me."

She inclined her head at him. "What do you mean? *A man like you.* You speak as though you are a dull sort of fellow, which is the farthest thing from the truth. Your work is fascinating. I am sure Mother would love to hear about your latest research. She is very much looking forward to our walk in the park tomorrow. The coachman will take us to the Marble Arch entrance around two o'clock, I believe. I do hope it will be a fair day. If it rains, we will hold off until the following day, but two o'clock is such a fine time to walk in the park, don't you agree? And the Marble Arch is a convenient spot to begin. It is not far from here."

Dr. Thomas inclined his head and studied her with some curiosity.

Charlotte forced herself to stop talking, for she was quite sure her subtlety had just slipped from her grip like a wet frog and was hopping like mad out the open window.

"Are you trying to play the matchmaker, Charlotte?" he asked with an amused look on his face.

She found herself relaxing, and chuckled softly as she dropped her gaze. "There it is. My secret is out. You know me too well, I suppose. I thought I could lure you innocently to the park, where you would take one look at Mother and remember what you were to each other at one time." Her gaze lifted. "You haven't seen her since the funeral. That was two years ago."

"How is she doing?" Dr. Thomas asked with a genuine note of compassion in his tone. "I know it wasn't easy for her in those final days before the duke slipped away."

"You were a great comfort to her," Charlotte told him, leaning forward to clasp and squeeze his hand on the desk. "I don't know what we would have done without you. Not just in those final days, but in all the years when he was so ..." She couldn't finish, for there were no proper words other than confused, delusional, impossible to care for. *Pitiful.*

"I was happy to be of service," Dr. Thomas said. "You know how much I care for you and your mother, and for all of your brothers."

Garrett especially—her twin—who like his father, was now a surgeon himself. The two men worked together occasionally at the medical school in London.

"I do know it," Charlotte replied, "which is why I have come. I would like to see Mother find happiness again. I thought perhaps you and she might like to spend some time together while she's in London."

"You have given this a lot of thought," he said with a smile.

"Yes," she openly admitted. "So what do you say? Could you join us tomorrow for a walk in the park?"

Dr. Thomas slowly pulled his hand from her grasp and sat back in his chair. He was quiet for a long moment, and his cool withdrawal caused a knot of discomfort to form in her belly.

"I appreciate the invitation," he said, "but I am afraid I must decline. I have appointments booked and I am sorry, Charlotte, but your Mother and I had our chance many years ago. She chose to marry the duke."

"But it wasn't really her choice," Charlotte argued. "I know what happened that night before the wedding. She only went through with her marriage to protect you."

"I didn't need her protection," he said. "All I wanted was *her*." Then he quickly shook his head, waved his hand as if to erase the conversation, and rose from his chair to stand in front of the window. "I don't want to discuss it any further. I care deeply for you and Adelaide, but please understand that I cannot pursue the very thing that nearly broke me on so many different occasions. I loved your mother and I dreamed of her for years, but then the time came for me to move on with my life and accept the fact that we were not meant to be together."

"But she is free at last," Charlotte argued as she watched him stare out the window with his hands clasped behind his back. "Won't you consider giving it one more try?"

He faced her. "I am sorry, Charlotte. I am Adelaide's friend now, but nothing more."

Charlotte stood up and approached him. "Please do not give up so easily. Things are different now. She is a widow. She can do as she wishes."

"And what is it, exactly, that she wishes to do?" he asked. "Do you even know?" He regarded Charlotte with a knitted brow. "Did she send you here? Or is this your idea, alone?"

Charlotte looked down at the floor. "She doesn't know I am here. I didn't want to push her—or you, for that matter. I had hoped we could simply encounter each other by accident at the park tomorrow."

"I see." He sat down on the window ledge and pinched the bridge of his nose. Then he looked up and inhaled deeply. "You must put this out of your mind, my dear. When I told you I had moved on with my life, I meant it. You say your mother is free at last, but the fact is ..." He paused. "I am not."

He may as well have thrown a glass of cold water in her face. Charlotte stepped back. "I don't understand."

He couldn't be married. She was his daughter. He would have told her. *Wouldn't he?*

"I have been courting someone," he said.

Charlotte swallowed uneasily. "Is there an agreement between you?" she asked as a sickening mixture of dread and disbelief flooded into her stomach. "Do you intend to marry her?"

"That is the direction it has been heading for quite some time," he replied. "She is a lovely woman—also a widow—and completely devoted to me. I have been a disappointed bachelor all my life, but she adores me, Charlotte. I hope you can be happy for me."

Charlotte looked into her father's eyes and felt a painful, aching love in her heart. Of course she wanted him to be happy, but she had wanted a happily ever after for herself as well. She had believed she could accomplish that by watching her true parents come together at last, fall in love all over again, and walk down the aisle while the family threw white flower petals at their feet.

But clearly that was not to be.

Somehow Charlotte found the strength to smile and take hold of his hand. "Of course I am happy for you," she said. "And I hope to meet this woman one day soon. She must be very special."

"I believe so," he said. "But let us take it one day at a time, shall we? I will introduce you when the time is right." He moved to fetch his spectacles from the desk. "Now I must see a patient, my dear."

"Of course. I will take my leave." Charlotte gathered up her reticule from the chair.

A few minutes later, she was standing outside on the breezy street, fighting a severe feeling of disappointment, and waving to her coachman who had parked a few doors down. How many years had she dreamed of seeing her parents finally reunited? The tragedy of their love affair always seemed so unfinished. She had genuinely believed a happy ending was possible for them.

Perhaps trying to play the matchmaker was her way of dealing with her own lost love. Perhaps, by bringing her parents back together, she would have been able to prove that the cracks and breaks in one's heart could be repaired one day. But it was not to be, and she was terribly unsettled by that awareness. She had been so sure that William and Adelaide would end up together. Was she truly a foolish dreamer? Was she living in a fantasy world?

The coach pulled up in front of her. She was about to step inside and return to Pembroke House when a giant lump formed in her throat. Good Lord. She couldn't possibly face her mother until she collected herself.

She turned to her driver. "I'm afraid I am not ready to go back yet. I would like to take a walk." She pointed down the street. "I'll just go to that corner and turn up that street there. I'll be back here in a quarter of an hour."

"Would you like George to accompany you?" the coachman asked.

The footman stepped forward. "It would be my pleasure, my lady."

She gave him an appreciative smile. "Thank you, but I would prefer to be alone with my thoughts. I shan't be long."

With that, she started down the street and turned at the corner.

It was a quiet residential neighborhood into which she ventured, and she strode at a brisk pace along the cement walk, looking around at the townhouses and wondering who lived in them—anything to take her mind off her botched attempt at matchmaking, and the fact that her parents were never going to be together.

Then suddenly, rapid footsteps pounded along the pavement behind her. She stopped to look back, wondering if there was some sort of emergency. Before she had a chance to make sense of the man who was barreling toward her, he grabbed hold of her reticule.

"What are you doing?" she cried as she gripped the purse tighter, refusing to let go.

The thief tugged harder and nearly swung her around. "Let go of it!" he shouted.

"I will not!" she replied as she leaned back to pull with all her might.

Charlotte had been raised with four brothers who were not above playing rough with her when they were children, and for that reason she was made of stern stuff. Nevertheless, she was completely astonished when the man shoved her back into the wrought iron fence in front of the closest townhouse. Her head snapped back and a sharp pain resonated in her skull. She was barely aware of her knees buckling as the world spun circles in front of her eyes, and she crumpled to the ground in a haze of white.

Chapter Three

*D*RAKE TORRINGTON WAS JUST exiting his townhouse when the sound of a lady's voice from across the street drew his attention.

"I will not!" she screamed.

He spotted her as she was knocked into the fence by a scoundrel who made off with her purse.

Drake leaped down the steps, darted across the street, and reached the woman in a matter of seconds. "Are you hurt?" he asked, kneeling down to lay a hand on her shoulder, for she had collapsed.

She seemed dazed by the strike to the head, but then she frowned up at him with a pair of gleaming blue eyes that upset his balance, for he hadn't seen a woman so beautiful in years—perhaps ever.

"I am fine, thank you, sir," she said as she struggled to rise, "but that man has stolen my reticule. I want it back."

He helped her to her feet. "You're certain you are all right?"

"Yes."

"Wait here, then." He took off after the thief who had paused foolishly at the corner to rummage through the contents of the purse.

Drake sprinted toward him. The man looked up in surprise, then turned to make a run for it.

Reaching into his pocket, Drake grabbed his watch—a conveniently heavy piece of gold weaponry—and pitched it at the back of the man's head.

The strike was spot on. The bandit tripped and tumbled forward to the ground. Disoriented, he rose up on his hands and knees and shook his head like a wet dog just as Drake came upon him, grabbed him by the lapels, and pulled him to his feet.

Drake shook him. "Hand it over, scoundrel, or I'll knock your brains out."

The thief refused to part with it. He threw a flimsy punch, which by some dumb stroke of luck connected with Drake's jaw. The pain reverberated through his skull and sparked his blood into red-hot flames of savage aggression.

It had been years since Drake had enjoyed a good fight, and he wondered what happened to his old instincts, for there was once a time he would have anticipated and easily skirted such a watered-down blow. His pride bucked violently in response, and a heartbeat or two later, the thief was sprawled out, unconscious, on the pavement while Drake stood over him, feet braced apart, flexing his bloodied fist.

The noises of the street had somehow faded away. All he could hear was the heavy beating of his own heart, like a continuous rumble of thunder in his ears.

As his body rhythms returned to a more natural pace, reality came crashing back. He dropped to his knees to check the man's pulse at his neck. He was still alive, thank God. Drake removed the reticule from the man's possession, rose to his feet, and turned around to discover the lady with the disarming blue eyes stood only a few feet away, staring at him in shock.

༄ぐ乙ひ༂

Charlotte felt slightly dizzy and considerably alarmed as she locked gazes with the man who had retrieved her reticule. Naturally, she was grateful that he had come to her rescue, but after witnessing such a shocking display of violence, she felt no safer now than she had when the thief came upon her.

She had watched every heated second of the altercation, and had recognized the force behind the gentleman's blow. Her breath had hitched in her throat when the thief was propelled backward through the air, as if he had been rammed by a raging bull at full gallop.

Glancing down at her rescuer's big brawny fist and bloody knuckles, then down at the lifeless form on the ground behind him, she carefully asked, "Is he alive?" It would be a miracle if he were.

"Yes." The gentleman's voice was husky and low, barely more than a growl, and she was riveted to the spot. "I believe this is yours," he added as he stepped forward and held out her reticule.

Charlotte stood utterly still as he drew near, for she felt rather breathless. From a distance she had known he was a tall man, but now she could sense—and *feel*—the looming power of his massive male brawn. His chest was thick, his shoulders wide, though his torso narrowed down to slender hips and undoubtedly strong legs.

"And this must be yours," she replied, holding out his pocket watch, which she had picked up on the street a moment before. "It still appears to be working."

As they made the exchange, Charlotte felt a shiver move through her. She wasn't sure what caused it. She told herself there was nothing to fear from this man who had subdued her attacker. Judging by the way he was dressed in a fine black frock coat, silk top hat, and shiny black shoes, he was a gentleman.

Nevertheless, her head was spinning like a top, for there was very little about him beyond his clothing that seemed the least bit refined. He was coarse looking, like a laborer. Crude, even. And perhaps it was the way he moved—with a dangerous swagger—that seemed particularly threatening after what she had just witnessed.

Or perhaps it was his rugged facial features. His eyes were a pale shade of blue-gray, his nose was misshapen, as if it might have been broken a few times in the past, and there were scars on his cheekbones, and evidence of an old gash through one of his eyebrows. His upper lip was scarred as well.

He reminded her of a barbarian from another time. She could easily imagine it—this man, with his huge, scarred, muscled body, standing shirtless in battle, swinging a sword in one hand, wielding a dagger in the other, his eyes burning with bloodlust. He was perfect …

Stop it, Charlotte.

"That was quite a punch," she said. "How is your hand?"

He flexed it a few times and looked down at his bloodied knuckles. His fingers were thick. So were his wrists. "It's fine."

"It doesn't look fine to me," she replied. "I daresay you did some damage, on both sides." She looked up and down the quiet street. "Should we send for someone? A constable perhaps? Or a doctor?" The side of her head was throbbing. A bump was probably forming already.

"I was thinking the same thing," he said in that husky, mesmerizing voice. "I live just there." He pointed at his townhouse, a few doors down. "If you will accompany me, madam, I will send one of my servants to fetch assistance, and I promise this man will be arrested."

"Is it wise to leave him here?" Charlotte asked. "What if he wakes up and runs off?"

"I will have him brought inside."

Then his eyes narrowed with displeasure and he took a step closer.

For some reason, Charlotte quickly backed away, as if he had swung another punch, this time in her direction.

"You're hurt," he said, not appearing the least bit surprised that she had recoiled from him.

"No, I'm not," she insisted.

He pointed to a drop of blood on her collar, and only then did she notice a wet sensation on her scalp. The dizziness she experienced earlier suddenly made sense, and when she slid her gloved fingers into her upswept hair and felt a gash just over her ear, her stomach turned over. "I'm bleeding."

For the second time that day, the world turned white before her eyes, her knees buckled beneath her, and she began to sink toward the ground.

Though teetering on the muddled edges of consciousness, Charlotte was keenly aware of the man scooping her up into his arms—as if she weighed no more than a bolt of fabric—and carrying her toward his home.

Clinging tightly to the frame of his shoulders, she fought to stay awake and not faint in his arms. He was rock-solid beneath her hands, and his exotic spicy cologne smelled delectable. She warmed with appreciation and something else ...

He mounted his front steps lightly, with no effort at all, as if they were both floating on air, and his incredible virility had a strange, appealing effect on her. Every fiber of her being hummed with awareness, energy, and excitement. A bolt of fear whizzed through her veins too ... though perhaps it wasn't fear, but something else entirely. Something exhilarating ... something more heady, more dangerous. Indeed, even in her fantasies she had never projected anything quite like it.

"That's it," he whispered softly in her ear as he shifted her in his arms to rap the lion's head doorknocker. "Just hold on to me, darling. You'll be fine. My housekeeper will tend to you. One shouldn't ignore a head wound, you know. They can be serious."

She suspected he was making conversation to keep her conscious, but there was little danger of nodding off, for she didn't want to miss a single moment of this strangely thrilling ordeal.

Soon the door opened and Charlotte was carried into the house. She looked around at the walls, the floors, the staircase, and the pictures on the walls as she was conveyed into a cozy front parlor, decorated with deep colors and chintz fabrics.

Clearly this house did not lack a woman's touch. She wondered if the gentleman had a wife, and if so, was she at home? What would she say when she saw her husband carry a strange woman to the sofa and lay her down upon it?

The butler appeared—perhaps he was the one who opened the door—and followed them into the room. "Was there an accident?" he asked.

"Yes," her rescuer replied as he ensured Charlotte was settled comfortably on the soft cushions. "This woman was robbed, and she requires our assistance. Please send for Mrs. March and tell her to bring warm water, bandages, and a washcloth. Send Richard to fetch a constable, but not before he and Alfred bring the thief inside." He leaned closer to the butler and lowered his voice. "Tie him up in the kitchen."

"Yes, sir," the butler said, and left to fulfill his duties.

While the gentleman looked out the window to keep an eye on the thief, Charlotte attempted to rise up on her elbows, but felt a sudden wave of nausea.

"Don't try to get up," he said. "Wait for the housekeeper. She'll be here shortly." His gaze returned to the street.

Charlotte watched his cool gray eyes sparkle like silver in the sunlight. "If I am going to thank you properly," she said, "I should at least know your name."

He faced her, clasped his hands behind his back, and bowed slightly. "My apologies, madam. I am Drake Torrington."

"Torrington . . ." Her eyebrows drew together as she tried to place the name.

"My uncle is Earl Lidstone," he explained.

Ah. So he was a member of the aristocracy. She wanted to rise to her feet and introduce herself properly, but dared not move from her position.

"Your uncle's estate is near Brighton, is it not?" she asked.

"That is correct."

"I know of it. I visited there once, when I was a girl."

"Did you," he flatly said.

Curious to know more about him, she politely inquired, "Do you have a family, sir? A wife and children?"

"No, there is only my mother, who is mistress here. I am not married, and I have only just returned from America."

"How long were you away?"

He glanced down at her briefly, then returned his gaze to the window for a long moment while his chest rose and fell with a sigh. "Twelve years."

"I see," Charlotte replied hesitantly. "Are you here only to visit, Mr. Torrington, or do you intend to stay?"

"I'll be leaving at the end of the summer," he told her, seeming distracted. "There. A few of my servants are bringing your thief inside now."

"Is he conscious?" Charlotte asked, trying again to sit up. This time she felt somewhat recovered.

"See for yourself." Mr. Torrington held the curtain aside for her. She was able to look out the window behind the sofa.

The man was on his feet and walking, though he leaned heavily on the men on either side, who escorted him inside. "I will have Mrs. March examine him when she is through with you," Mr. Torrington said.

Charlotte regarded her rescuer curiously in the window's light as it reflected off his shiny black hair. Then she realized she had not yet told him her name. "Mr. Torrington, how do you do. I am Charlotte Sinclair of Pembroke." She held out her gloved hand. He bent forward to shake it.

"Pembroke Palace?"

"Yes. My eldest brother is the duke."

His eyebrows lifted. "You don't say. In that case, I am deeply honored to have been of assistance to you, Lady Charlotte."

Their eyes locked and held, and she felt a shock of awareness at the thrill of his touch. He had not yet let go of her hand, and she was astonished by the fact that he did not crush it—for she knew the size and strength of those brawny fists.

But there was something else, too, that she noticed—a curious and devilishly charming flicker of light in his eyes that sent a hot and rather explosive spark of attraction to her core.

Just then, the housekeeper entered the room, and Charlotte was forced to let go of his hand. He moved away rather quickly and said, "My lady, allow me to present Mrs. March. This is Lady Charlotte Sinclair of Pembroke Palace, and she has hit her head. Will you take a look at her?"

"I would be pleased to do so, sir," the housekeeper replied, and pulled a chair up to sit alongside the sofa. She set her bowl of water and cloths on the floor. "Now tell me, where does it hurt?" she asked.

Charlotte indicated the spot over and behind her ear.

"Ah yes ... You did some damage, I see. Did you lose consciousness?"

"I don't believe so, though I did feel very faint."

"Can you wiggle your feet for me?" Mrs. March asked while she examined the wound.

Charlotte wiggled her feet.

"What about double vision? Or numbness or tingling in your hands or feet?"

"No, nothing like that," Charlotte replied.

"Very good. Now let me see your pupils. Turn your face toward the light?" Charlotte did as she was told, and the housekeeper examined her eyes.

Turning toward Mr. Torrington, who had moved to the other side of the parlor, the housekeeper said, "She appears to be perfectly fine, sir. I'll just clean the wound now. It doesn't look like she needs stitches."

"That is excellent news," he replied. "Now, if you will both excuse me."

He left the room—no doubt to check on the thief who had been brought in through the servants' entrance downstairs—and Charlotte was left alone with the housekeeper. "Are you a nurse?" she asked. "You seem quite knowledgeable."

"I have some experience with head wounds, my lady. I know when it's serious enough to call the doctor."

"Where did you gain such useful knowledge?" she asked.

The housekeeper glanced down at her very briefly while she continued to clean Charlotte's wound. "That's not for me to say, my lady. You'll have to ask Mr. Torrington about that."

"I do beg your pardon. I didn't mean to pry."

Nothing more was said after that. Charlotte sat quietly and patiently while Mrs. March finished cleaning her wound. Only then did she realize that her coachman was probably very concerned, for she had been gone far longer than fifteen minutes.

When the housekeeper finished her duty, she collected up the bowl of water with bloody washcloth and returned the chair to its original position by the wall.

"I am grateful for your assistance," Charlotte said, "but I really must be on my way. My driver is probably beside himself with worry. I only meant to take a short walk."

"Is he nearby?" Mrs. March asked, crossing to the window to look out.

"He is waiting for me on Park Lane."

"Then you must wait for Mr. Torrington to escort you. Please do not get up too quickly, my lady, or you may feel faint again. I will go and fetch him."

"Thank you." Charlotte waited in the empty parlor while the clock ticked steadily on the mantel and her head throbbed.

When at last Mr. Torrington appeared in the doorway, she did exactly what Mrs. March warned her not to do, and stood up quickly. The room spun in circles before her eyes, but somehow she managed to maintain her balance.

"I was told you wish to be on your way," he said in that husky voice that slid over her like velvet.

"Yes, if you don't mind. I am sure my driver is quite worried."

"Of course." He strode to her, offered his arm, and she took it. A moment later, they were strolling out the door and descending the steps.

"The constable may wish to speak with you," Mr. Torrington said. "May I have permission to tell him your name and where you live?"

"Absolutely," she replied. "I will be at Pembroke House in Mayfair. He may come by today if he wishes, as I intend to go straight home."

They walked along the sunbathed street, Charlotte's heels clicking sharply on the pavement. She was very aware of Mr. Torrington's muscled arm beneath her hand and his breathtaking masculine presence beside her.

It had not been a good day. In fact, it had been one of the worst days in recent memory, yet her body was sizzling with excitement. She hadn't felt this alive in years and knew the reason for it. It was more than the attack and the bump on the head. It was Mr. Torrington. She had never met anyone quite like him and she found herself wondering what it would be like to be held in his arms, to be kissed passionately by him in the dark, to lie naked with him on a hot summer night under the stars. Would he be gentle with a woman, or would he be rough?

Heaven help her, it had been a lifetime since she'd known true passion, and lately she felt as if her body would burst into flames if she did not enjoy the erotic pleasure of a man's touch again before she grew too old to want or need it.

She was a spinster. It was not likely she would ever marry, but why couldn't she take a lover? And why couldn't it be this handsome stranger? For he excited her. No one had excited her like this since Graham.

They reached the corner. Charlotte spotted her coach and driver still waiting at the curb not far from Dr. Thomas's office. She stopped and turned to face Mr. Torrington. "I cannot thank you enough," she said, "for your gallant rescue today, and for retrieving my reticule. Please thank Mrs. March for her kind attention."

"I will," he replied.

"My coach is just there, so I shall walk the rest of the way on my own. But before I go, I wish to say something, and I suspect it may shock you."

"Yes?" He inclined his head slightly.

She hesitated. "I would like to see you again, Mr. Torrington. In private."

Had she really said it? Yes, she had.

His silvery blue gaze dipped lower, to her mouth, then slowly, knowingly lifted back up to her eyes. "For what purpose, Lady Charlotte?"

He was a man of few words, but there was something about him that required very few of them. Something sultry and seductive. Physically powerful.

"You mentioned you were unmarried," she boldly said. "I, too, am unattached. You are here for the Season. So am I. Perhaps we could ... become better acquainted."

The corner of his mouth curled up in a small grin that made her knees go all buttery soft. "Do you wish to thank me again?" he asked.

"Yes, I do."

She never imagined she would speak so scandalously to a man, but this one was not like other London gentlemen. He had been living in America for the past twelve years. Doing what ...? She had no idea. And he would be returning there soon. He was also rather rough and unrefined. He was not a member of her social circle, yet he was the nephew of an earl.

If she were ever going to take a secret lover, was he not an excellent choice? If things did not work out, he would soon be gone—but most importantly, he excited her. He was like some sort of battle-roughened Roman gladiator in city clothes. He could be the perfect fulfillment of her fantasy.

"Then I am at your service, my lady," he replied with a small bow.

Charlotte squeezed her reticule in her hands, for she wasn't entirely sure how this was done. "Do you walk in the park at the fashionable hour?" she asked. "Or do you attend the theater?"

"I do neither of those things," he replied, not making this easy on her at all.

"Why ever not?"

He squinted toward the park as he answered. "Because I intend to remain on the fringes of Society while I am in Town."

Even more perfect. But also odd, so she posed another question. "May I ask why?"

His eyes met hers again, and there was a hint of a smile in them—a flicker of playful flirtation and encouragement. "I wouldn't venture to bore you with it, Lady Charlotte. It's rather tedious," he explained.

"I see." He did not want to share the story of his life with her, but he did not wish to reject her either, and she understood why, for she could feel the attraction sparking between them in the scorching heat of the afternoon. Her body began to perspire, and she felt a rather pleasant ache in the pit of her belly and between her thighs—from just looking at him.

She raised a coquettish eyebrow. "I doubt anything about you could be tedious," she said, and felt the heat between them escalate. "But I will honor your wishes and ask no more questions. At least not today. Except for this *one*. What *do* you like to do, Mr. Torrington? When and how can we meet? On the fringes, as you say."

This was all scandalously improper and not at all prudent. Here was a stranger she had just met—a man who had, a short while ago, punched another man with such brutal force, he was left seeing stars—and she was suggesting they meet alone, outside the bounds of good Society? *Was she mad?* Yes, she supposed so.

At the moment, she was mad with desire. That had to explain where this urgency was coming from.

Something about him had gotten under her skin and into her blood. The need for this man was unlike anything she had ever known and the draw of it crushed all reason and any inhibitions.

"I row on the Thames every morning at dawn."

No wonder his hands were huge and callused and his arms were so thickly muscled.

"Is there room in your boat for two?" she asked.

"Yes, if you are the adventurous sort."

She smiled. "I grew up in the country with four brothers, Mr. Torrington. I assure you, I have no fear of adventure."

"Then I will bring my coach around and pick you up at Pembroke House at six," he said.

"I will look forward to it."

He began to back away. "Take care of that pretty head, Lady Charlotte"

A wicked thrill moved through her at the compliment, and she smiled to herself as she, too, reluctantly backed away to return to her coach.

Chapter Four

*D*RAKE WAS NOT IN the habit of inviting attractive
women along for his morning exercise. It was a
time of day he preferred to keep for himself, though he
supposed most times of the day fell into that category,
for he was not a social person. He had retreated from
the world many years ago and chose to live a very
private life.

That did not mean he was a complete recluse,
however, and he was certainly not a celibate monk.
He often took a lover for a sustained period of time,
a few months at least or even a year if the lady was
particularly amiable and did not expect too much from
him—meaning marriage, of course, or a certain level
of togetherness to which he was not willing to commit.
He preferred independent women who had their own
interests beyond his attentions. Women who were
intelligent, who possessed a good wit—and it certainly
didn't hurt if they were beautiful. Though it was not
a requirement.

One of his most enjoyable affairs had been with
a woman who was not tall, blond, or statuesque.
Her hair was red, her cheeks were freckled, and her
nose was too large, but she was always smiling and

she understood Drake's temperament. She made him laugh and cared nothing for the latest fashions or society gossip. In a way, she'd been an outsider, like him, and they'd had a good time together while it lasted and remained friends to this day.

Lady Charlotte of Pembroke Palace was nothing like her, however, for she was tall, blond, and statuesque, with an ivory complexion, full lips like sweet ripe cherries, and eyes that, when focused on him, nearly knocked him backward. Everything about her—the fashionable gown, the silk shoes, and ridiculous plumed hat—screamed money and rank. She was not Drake's preferred type at all. Yet here he sat, pulling up in front of her family's London residence at dawn, wondering if he should get out and knock on the door, or wait for her like a secret, forbidden paramour in the shadows.

This was strange indeed. They had barely spoken more than a few words to each other before she presented her scandalous offer to thank him again. Perhaps that's what made it so titillating. He found himself unable to resist testing how far this would go.

He sat forward in his seat and peered out the window at the house, then reached into his pocket for his watch. It was not quite six o'clock. How long would he wait if she did not appear? Perhaps she had come to her senses and changed her mind. Perhaps she had thought more carefully about the way he had chased down her thief and beaten him insensible. If so, Drake would simply move on, enjoy his morning exercise, and think no more about her.

The front door of the house opened just then and Lady Charlotte walked out.

Drake flung the door of the coach open and stepped out to greet her. "Good morning," he said, surprised by how good it made him feel that she had kept her word.

"Good morning to you," she cheerfully replied as she placed her gloved hand in his and allowed him to assist her into the dimly lit interior of the vehicle. When they were comfortably seated across from each other, she said, "I wasn't sure if you would really come. I thought I might have dreamed all of that yesterday."

"How is your head?" he asked as he rapped his walking stick on the roof and the coach moved on.

"Much better, thank you. A good night's sleep did the trick."

"In my experience, it always does. It's a cure for a great many maladies."

"Well said." There was something lively about her this morning. She seemed invigorated. Obviously the early morning hours agreed with her.

"Did the constable come to see you?" Drake asked.

"Yes, about an hour after I arrived home. I told him everything that happened, and he wrote it all down." She gazed out the window. "I hope they are not too hard on the man. I hate to think that he might have been desperate, merely trying to feed his family."

"That wasn't the case," Drake assured her. "He is a single man with a gambling problem and owed money to the wrong people. But your forgiveness does you credit, Lady Charlotte, considering how he caused you such injury. You were lucky. Head wounds are unpredictable. It could have been much worse."

She turned her eyes toward him again, and he felt his body flex. God, she truly was astonishingly beautiful, almost too beautiful to look at.

What exactly did she want from him? He studied her as they traveled in the gently swaying coach. Was it presumptuous of him to assume it was something wicked? Something private and pleasurably depraved, when surely, she could have any man she wanted?

Funny, this was not the first time a woman like her had propositioned him. The glitzy ones sometimes enjoyed a brief roll in the gutter with a man like him, for he knew what kind of impression he made. On the surface he appeared rough and uncultivated. There was something about his looks—the facial scars, the way he spoke, and carried himself—that drew women's attention. He knew he didn't fit into the glittering ballrooms and pretentious drawing rooms of the English upper classes, despite that fact that he was fifth in line to an earldom.

"Tell me, Mr. Torrington," she said, leaning back in a lushly sensual way, "what should I expect from our excursion today? How big is your boat?"

"It's not the size of the boat that matters," he replied, "but the skill of the oarsman. A sleek hull can make a difference as well."

Her tongue darted out to lick her lips, and he felt another surge of rather hedonistic lust that moved from his mind to his groin.

"I suspect your skill with the oars is first-rate, Mr. Torrington, since you row each morning. Practice makes perfect, they say. How fast will we go? Am I dressed all right? Or will I lose my hat out on the water?"

"You are dressed perfectly, Lady Charlotte, and I will move as fast, or slow, as you desire. I can do both equally well." He looked her over seductively.

"I am sure that you can."

Their gazes remained fixed on each other's while she twirled a lock of hair at her temple. She fiddled with it in a deliberately suggestive manner, and he wondered what the bloody hell he was getting himself into.

He had come home to ensure that his mother would be taken care of in the years to come, not to become involved in a scorching hot love affair with a woman who could turn out to be very manipulative and demanding. He suspected she'd practiced that hair-twirling gesture in front of a mirror. He knew nothing about her deeper character. She could be one of those spoiled, possessive types who throw china vases when things don't go their way. Heaven help them both if that turned out to be the case.

The coach rumbled noisily over the city cobblestones on the way to the river jetty where he kept his boat.

"If you don't mind me asking," she said, "what kept you in America for so long? Did you intend to stay there permanently when you first crossed the Atlantic?"

"Permanently is too strong a word," he replied. "I only knew that I wouldn't return for a long while."

"And what is it that you do there? Forgive the questions, but I have always wanted to visit America. It sounds so very modern and progressive."

"Yes," he said. "It is not like it is here. Americans are not so steeped in senseless tradition. At least most of them are not. The country is only just finding its legs, and I have enjoyed being a part of that growing awareness."

"How so?"

The questions were taking a personal turn, but he had no reason to keep anything secret about his life abroad, so he spoke openly.

"I am a railroad investor," he explained.

"Really?" She sat forward. "How fascinating."

"I like to think so," he agreed. "The varying geography of the country is overwhelming. The American frontier stretches for thousands of miles, and there are mountains, prairies, and lakes the size of small oceans. At one time, it seemed impossible to imagine that there could be a way to connect the two coasts, but the railroad is changing everything. Commerce is booming. The possibilities there are endless."

"It must be very exciting to be a part of that."

It had been both exciting and lucrative, for he had traveled to America with a significant fortune, and had quadrupled it three times over since his departure twelve years ago. He was probably richer than her brother the duke, but he was not the sort to flaunt his wealth.

"But it must have also been exciting to return home after such a long time away," she added. "I am sure your mother was pleased to see you."

He shrugged at that, for he and his mother were not close. Not in the least. As her only living son, he was here merely to do his duty by her. Then he would be gone again.

"It appears we have arrived," he said as the coach pulled to a halt not far from the water's edge. Drake flicked the latch and pushed the coach door open, then stepped out and offered his hand.

"It's not too late to change your mind," he said, reluctantly releasing her fingers. "You could wait here if you prefer not to get wet."

"Why? Do you intend to sink us?"

"I don't intend to," he replied with some amusement, "but there is always some unintentional splashing, and the water is chilly."

"I shall weather it, Mr. Torrington," she said as he led her to the jetty, "but I appreciate your concern for my welfare."

༄༅༅

Mr. Torrington stepped into the rowboat and held out his hand to her. As she joined him, the boat pitched and rolled. She quickly took a seat on the bench at the stern.

"It's a very nice boat," she said, noting that it was only recently built, for she could smell the freshness of the wood.

Torrington untied the ropes. He sat down, removed his coat, set it aside, and picked up the oars. By braking with one oar and pulling with the other, he turned the small rowboat around to head out onto the river.

There was not a single breath of wind, and the water was as still as glass. A hint of mist hovered over its surface. Charlotte closed her eyes, breathed in the fresh morning air, and listened to the sounds of the oars dipping into the water. The boat thrust firmly forward with each stroke, and when she opened her eyes, she was astonished by the speed at which they were traveling.

Mr. Torrington, dressed in a loose white shirt and black waistcoat, was already breaking into a sweat. Then he began to row even faster. Charlotte could not fail to notice his big hands gripping the oar handles with tremendous might, and the strength of his legs as he braced them and propelled the boat forward. She also noticed that his knuckles were scabbed from the fight the previous day.

"You're very good at this," she said, amazed at the power of his strokes. The boat cut through the water's surface like a blade.

"It's a favorite pastime of mine," he said.

"Do you race?"

"Yes," he replied, crunching forward to perform another impressive stroke. "Whitehall racing is quite the thing in Boston and New York."

"Whitehall ...?"

"The name of this type of rowboat. Some say it originated in England, but others argue that it is an American design."

Charlotte was not sure what she had expected from today. She thought she'd seen it all when she watched Mr. Torrington knock a man out in the street, but now, in an entirely different set of circumstances, she was spellbound yet again ... by his broad shoulders in that loose white shirt, his massive biceps flexing, and his raw masculinity. He was a giant of a man, brimming with a magnetism that caused her body to shiver with excitement and promise. He made her feel hungry for something ... beyond propriety. She imagined throwing herself onto his lap, wrapping her arms around his neck, and devouring him with slow, deep kisses that lasted until noon.

She'd never felt such raw attraction before. No man had ever aroused her desires in such a way, and she knew that she simply had to have him. He was the one. She was as certain of that as if she'd selected him from inside a glass case at the jewelry shop.

"How far do you go each morning?" she asked, working to distract herself from thoughts of those big hands roaming over her bare skin.

"I row hard and fast for a quarter of an hour." He practically grunted out the words. "Then I slow down and turn back, and return at a more leisurely pace."

Her head nearly snapped back with the force of each thrust of the oars. "You're very strong," she said with a laugh.

Glancing over his shoulder briefly, he gave no reply. She could see he was focused on achieving greater speed and ensuring the right direction.

His hair had grown damp with perspiration, and was unruly. He flicked his head to toss it back out of his eyes. His shirt stuck to his shoulders. Shiny beads of sweat were visible on his chest where his shirt collar was open. What she wouldn't give to lick the dampness off his neck as she imagined she would do if he were her lover. Lord in heaven, she had never before, in her real life, entertained such wicked thoughts about a man.

She felt perspiration on her forehead as well, but not from any physical exertion. She sat primly with both hands on the gunwale, but felt all tangled up inside, mesmerized and craving to be closer to his potent masculinity.

When they reached the end of the quarter hour, he stopped rowing, lifted the oars out of the water, and paused to catch his breath. It was at that moment he met her gaze, while his chest heaved and the boat slowly drifted to a halt.

They floated freely for a moment or two. He leaned back, rested his elbows on another bench behind him, and grimaced. "I am afraid I'm not much of a conversationalist this early in the morning. Are you bored?"

Was he joking?

"Far from it," she replied. "This is tremendous. I am riveted. You have my attention, all of it." Her heart was racing and her body was on fire with exhilaration and anticipation.

He took another moment to recover his breathing, then sat up and turned the boat around.

"Will this be the leisurely portion of the tour?" she asked.

He smiled and nodded. "Yes, it's time to slow things down."

She suspected she was going to like it slow, just as well as fast.

"Lady Charlotte, tell me," he said. "What were you doing in my neighborhood yesterday, all on your own?"

She couldn't very well confess that she had gone to visit her real father to try and pair him up with her mother, or that she had failed miserably and needed to be alone because she was brokenhearted. Hence, she steered the conversation elsewhere.

"I had a meeting with my publisher yesterday, and I needed to work through some ideas."

He leaned forward, then pushed back with those strong legs for a long, slow stroke of the oars. "Are you a writer?"

"Yes. A novelist."

"You don't say." He glanced over his shoulder. "Would I know your work?"

"Possibly. My book has been selling well in America, they tell me."

"What's it called?"

She hesitated, for she had been using a *nom de plume*. "I write under a man's name," she said. "My publisher felt the book would sell better that way. It's Victor Edwards."

He immediately stopped rowing. "Are you having me on?"

"No." She chuckled.

"*You're* Victor Edwards?"

"Yes."

The boat began to drift on the current. "I am sitting in my boat with Victor Edwards. *The* Victor Edwards. And he's a woman?"

"That's right."

He stared at her. "I am in shock!"

Charlotte laughed again. "So you've heard of me, then?"

He slowly resumed rowing. "Yes, and I've read your book. It was quite ..." He paused.

She hated when people paused like that. She always feared it was because they hated it, and didn't know how to politely say so.

"Quite ...?" She drew a circle in the air to encourage him to hurry and find the right word.

"It was well researched," he said.

"Ah. So you didn't like it."

"No, you mistake me. I enjoyed the story very much. I was particularly interested in the main character—Jesse."

"The boxer," she said. It was also the title of the book.

"Yes." He glanced over his shoulder again, then shook his head in disbelief.

"What do you find so amusing?" she asked. "There is something you're not telling me."

He faced her again and lifted the oars out of the water. "I read the book because the title captured my attention. I am a boxer myself, you see. Well ... a retired boxer."

"Not professional, though," she said, for he was a gentleman, the nephew of an earl. It was not uncommon for young noblemen to dabble in the sport, but it was quite another matter to earn one's living in the ring.

"I was," he said, surprising her with his reply. "And I made a small fortune at it, too."

"I don't doubt it, based on what I witnessed yesterday. Is that why you went to America in the beginning? To fight over there?"

He adjusted the oars in the oarlocks then dipped them into the water again. "No, I boxed here in England. I only went to America after I decided to quit the sport."

Charlotte sat speechless while she did the math. He had told her yesterday that he had been gone for twelve years, which would have put him in the ring in 1875, or so.

She had indeed done a significant amount of research for her novel and had read about many of England's professional boxers. One in particular had gained notoriety as a champion until he suddenly went missing from the news. There was some speculation that he had been murdered, but a body was never discovered, so the case was closed.

"Forgive me for asking this question, Mr. Torrington," she said, "but are you ... were you ... The Iron Fist?"

The Iron Fist was one of the most celebrated, and feared sportsmen in the country who managed to keep his true identity a secret. Any man brave enough to step into the ring with him subjected himself to incomprehensible violence. They didn't call him The Iron Fist for nothing, and eventually the boxing establishment had trouble finding sparring partners for him, for no one dared go head to head with him. He had never been defeated.

Mr. Torrington's eyes narrowed, as if he were impressed by her clever deduction. She supposed not many women would have knowledge of such things.

"It appears we have something in common, Lady Charlotte," he said. "We both have stage names, so to speak. Though your profession is far more civilized than mine ever was."

Charlotte blinked at him. "I am astonished."

"So am I," he replied. "What are the odds I would end up in a row boat with Victor Edwards, who had clearly based much of his main character on *me*."

"That is *not* true," she quickly said in her defence. "Jesse was a composite of a number of different boxers, and the circumstances of his life were born out of my imagination. You must admit, your situations are not the same at all. Jesse gets a happy ending, while you simply disappeared. Good gracious. You were in America all this time? Why was your disappearance such a mystery? Was there anyone who knew what happened to you?"

"My family and a few close friends knew the truth," he explained.

Charlotte remembered how his housekeeper had been so knowledgeable about head wounds on the day Charlotte was robbed. "Mrs. March must have tended to your injuries more than once," she said. "Now I understand why she was so secretive about her skills."

"Yes, and if you don't object, Lady Charlotte, I would appreciate it if you could refrain from mentioning my presence here to anyone. I wish to keep my privacy."

She looked out over the still waters. "I will keep your secret if you will keep mine," she replied. "For the very same reason. I do not wish to be famous. I only want to live a normal, quiet life, and write stories."

"About boxers?"

She smiled at him. "No. The next book is about an orphan boy who is taken in by gypsies, and later discovers his real father is not dead, as he was led to believe. He is a high court judge and his mother was one of the judge's housemaids, who was murdered after giving birth."

"By whom?"

"By the judge's wife."

"My word," he said. "Have you no mercy, Lady Charlotte? Your poor, unfortunate characters. Does this one have a happy ending, at least for the boy?"

"I haven't decided yet," she replied, "for I have only just begun."

"Then I will look forward to reading it when it is finished."

ᘯᘓᘮ

As soon as Drake secured the boat to the jetty, he shrugged back into his jacket and offered his arm to Lady Charlotte.

He always felt revitalized after his early morning exercise, but today was different from all the other days, for his body was smoldering with a level of desire he had not felt in years.

Surely, there was a simple explanation for it, he told himself, for Lady Charlotte was a beautiful woman with soft full lips, hypnotic eyes, and abundant curves in all the right places. Even the silky tone of her voice made his body tremble, made him want to smother her words with his mouth and devour her whole.

But that was not the whole story. Discovering that she was Victor Edwards—a successful novelist, but also a woman who knew a thing or two about a boxer's life, and somehow, miraculously understood a violent man's soul—seemed to heighten his attraction to her.

For the first time he had revealed his past to a woman who would likely become his lover. It was not conceit that led him to expect such an affair to occur. Lady Charlotte had been more than candid with her words, her actions, and her eyes. He saw the way she looked at him ... how her gaze raked admiringly over the length of his body, how her hands stroked over her clothes whenever their eyes locked and held. There was a shared sexual desire between them, that required consummation.

In addition, this morning, something new had entered the equation. He had believed initially that she was a bored member of the aristocracy who wanted him for a few weeks of idle pleasure, to satisfy some wicked fantasy about a savage man who would remain outside her social circle and not taint her reputation with the roughness of his hands.

But Lady Charlotte was not idle or bored. How could she be, when her mind was occupied by the composition of lengthy tragic novels? He had read her book. There was depth to her characters, but where did her awareness of such people come from? How could this privileged woman write about such struggle without knowing something of it herself? As he did.

He was curious now. He wanted to peel back the layers and open her up. In more ways than one.

As they entered the coach and settled into their seats—this time he sat beside her, not across from her—he watched her with passionate interest and delicious anticipation.

"That was most enjoyable Mr. Torrington," she said, folding her gloved hands upon her lap and looking up at him with tantalizing, gleaming eyes.

"Yes, it was."

As the coach moved forward up the rutted lane, his thigh bumped hers and continued to rub against it. The press of her hip against his own quickly flooded him with arousal, which made him resent the fact that he must behave as a gentleman, for she was the daughter of a duke, and he wasn't entirely sure she knew what she had asked for. Until he knew for sure, he must continue to obey the rules, at least for the moment. But damn, how he wanted to forgo such social strictures and touch her now, in a most improper way.

His heart pounded in his chest and thrust hot blood through his veins like a violent force of nature. For a long moment, he refrained from looking at her, though he could feel her eyes on his profile.

"Are you nervous?" he asked, looking the other way so as not to arouse his desires any further. At least not yet.

"Should I be?" Her voice was both innocent and seductive. It sent another surge of lust to his loins.

At last, he turned to meet her gaze. "Yes."

"Why?"

"Because we are alone, Lady Charlotte, and you must know what I am thinking about. What I want."

"And what is that, Mr. Torrington?" she asked, as if she'd rehearsed the words a thousand times.

She knew damn well what it was. The flirtatious flash of light in her eyes gave her away, and Drake found himself more deeply aroused than before.

He leaned closer to take her mouth in a passionate kiss, but hesitated just before their lips met, for he needed to know that he had her consent. That he was not mistaken. That she wanted this, too.

He felt the heat of her sweet breath on his mouth. Then she lifted her face so the morning sun reflected in her clear eyes.

It was enough to push him over the cliff edge of desire, and when he pressed his mouth to hers, his hard body shuddered with yearning.

A single kiss was not going to be enough. Not nearly enough.

Her mouth was warm and wet and eager for sensual play. Her tongue darted out to meet his, and he groaned with need.

It had not been that long since he kissed a woman, but something about this encounter had been different from the beginning. He felt like an untried schoolboy, desperate for a taste of a real flesh-and-blood woman with soft skin and warm hands to pleasure him. He was completely overpowered, out of control, enormously aroused to the point of agony.

The coach continued to bump along the narrow road and Drake could see no reason to withdraw. Without ever breaking the kiss, Lady Charlotte pulled off her gloves and laid her hands on his cheeks. She shifted her body on the seat to face him, and he, too, shifted to gain better access to her delicious mouth.

He slid a hand over her hip and under her sweet backside to lift her legs across his lap. She yielded beautifully to the new position.

Before long, she was sighing with ecstasy and clutching at his shoulders, but he wanted her on her back, and realized with a sudden pang of consciousness that this kiss had spun out of control very quickly.

He dragged his mouth from hers, while a hot shiver of loss rippled down his spine.

"Please don't stop," she breathlessly said. "We don't have to yet."

They were still some distance from Mayfair, and though he wanted to maintain control, her passionate plea bombarded his senses. He gave in without a fight.

As if to make up for time, her hands roamed quickly, searched over his shoulders, chest, arms, and hips, then slid back up to his hair. He began to perspire and shake, for he had a giant erection that was throbbing like a son of a bitch.

He really should stop this now, or he would soon be making love to Lady Charlotte right here in the coach—though perhaps that was what she wanted.

Was it what *he* wanted? He certainly didn't want to be rushed.

"Stop," he said, bringing the kiss to a rather sloppy finish and holding her away at arm's length. "Not here." He wanted to do this properly, and do it well. "Meet me tonight."

She blinked up at him as if in a foggy haze, fighting to catch her breath. "Where?"

He considered it for a moment, pleased, of course that there was no argument, but at a loss as to how to answer the question. He didn't want to take her to the opera or invite her to dinner, and he suspected she didn't want those things either. She wanted him as a lover—in private—as he wanted her. They'd already pushed beyond the boundaries of any sort of polite courtship. They wanted each other's bodies. That was obvious, and it had been obvious from the start. On top of all that, this was guaranteed to be a brief sexual affair, for he was in London for a limited time and she knew it.

"At the Harper Hotel," he said. "There is an entrance at the rear of the building where you can enter discreetly. No one will see you. I will have the room key, and I will be there just inside the door to meet you." When she gave no reply, he drew back slightly. "Have I presumed too much, Lady Charlotte?"

She shook her head. "No, but please allow me to explain that I have never done anything like this before. I have never in my life taken a casual lover."

He inhaled deeply with relief. *Casual lover.* There they were ... the words on her lips, spoken in plain terms. It was what they would be to each other. It represented consent, intention. A promise of temporary pleasure.

Then he pondered her declaration, and the underlying message he could glean from it. She claimed she had never taken a casual lover, but she was unmarried. She was not a twenty-year-old debutante. Was she a virgin?

He couldn't possibly ask the question. He'd already taken enough liberties this morning, which left him curious and intrigued.

Was he to be her first? Or was there some other story?

The coach turned onto the main road. Drake forced himself to sit back and allow Lady Charlotte a few moments to collect herself before they reached Mayfair, for it had been an unexpectedly heated ride from the jetty.

"I will accept your invitation," she said as she tucked a few loose strands of hair up under her hat. "What time?"

"Can you be there at midnight?" he asked.

"I can do anything I want," she replied with a wicked grin that made him want to leap across this seat and take her right then and there.

"And is this truly what you want?" he asked.

The coach pulled to a halt in front of Pembroke House.

"Oh, yes," she replied, leaning close and touching her lips lightly to his. They were soft and smiling, and he smiled in return as she drew away and slid alluringly toward the coach door.

"What have you done to me, Mr. Torrington?" she playfully asked as he reached past her to flick the door latch and push it open.

"Nothing yet," he said. "But summer has only just begun."

"And I have the utmost confidence that we will make the most of it."

With that, she slipped out of his coach, leaving him positively ravenous with anticipation for their forthcoming encounter.

Chapter Five

CHARLOTTE KNEW HER CHEEKS were flushed when she walked into the house and was greeted by the butler. She hoped he would consider her high color a consequence of the cool and dewy morning air, for it was not yet nine o'clock.

She handed over her hat and gloves and proceeded upstairs to the breakfast room for eggs and coffee, which she sorely needed to snap herself back to reality after the dreamlike seduction in Mr. Torrington's coach. It had been everything she'd wanted—and more.

She could barely fathom all that she had learned about him on the river, and all that he had revealed, much less what had occurred between them on the return trip. Charlotte had been wildly attracted to him from the first moment he swept her into his arms and carried her into his house. Watching him row the boat at high speed against the current of the river had only added heat to the flame, and the passionate kiss in the coach had sealed her fate.

Surely it would be impossible to resist a full-scale love affair with him, and to her utter delight, he had expressed a similar desire. *Expressed it with his body.* She had recognized his arousal for he had been wonderfully aggressive, breathing heavily, and touching her hungrily with those strong, sure hands.

Heaven help her, what should she expect tonight when she met him at the hotel? If she didn't lose her courage before then and change her mind completely.

Charlotte reached the top of the stairs and breathed in the scent of honey-smoked ham and coffee. After her thrilling boat ride on the river, she was famished.

"Good morning," Adelaide said as Charlotte entered and poured herself a cup of coffee.

Her mother had no notion that Charlotte had ventured out at six o'clock to meet a potential lover, so Charlotte served up a plate of eggs and ham, and sat down as if nothing were amiss.

"What are your plans for the day?" Adelaide asked as she set the newspaper down on the white tablecloth.

"Nothing."

"Didn't you mention that we might take a walk in the park? I would like to do something that does not involve crowds or shopping."

Charlotte set down her coffee cup. "Oh yes. Although Hyde Park is not the best place to go if you wish to avoid a crowd on a sunny afternoon."

"I will tolerate the crowds in exchange for green grass, birds, and trees," Adelaide replied. "Two o'clock, did you not say?"

Indeed, Charlotte had been quite adamant about that particular time of the day, for she had hoped to entice Dr. Thomas to join them. But since their discussion in his office the day before, the urgency to take her mother to the park had diminished with the news that Dr. Thomas was involved with another woman now.

"What about a museum or art gallery this afternoon?" Charlotte suggested. "I daresay it looks like rain."

The sky was a bright shade of blue, however, and the birds were singing.

"Don't be silly," Adelaide said. "It is a glorious day and I want to walk in the park and twirl our parasols. You look very fetching in your lavender walking gown, darling. Why not wear that one?"

Charlotte realized that her mother had come to London with high hopes that her daughter might at last meet a handsome gentleman worthy of stealing her heart. So ... Adelaide was playing matchmaker, too, though apparently she had not yet identified an appropriate suitor.

Charlotte considered mentioning that she had already selected a handsome man to enjoy for the summer. He was the famous retired boxer they called The Iron Fist, and it was going to be a purely sexual affair.

Swallowing uneasily, she set down her fork. "A walk in the park sounds delightful," she said, and finished her coffee without saying another word.

ღთღ

Contrary to Charlotte's prediction about an unexpected rainfall, the weather remained fine that afternoon. She and Adelaide opened their parasols and climbed into the barouche, which first took them for a drive through Piccadilly, then circled around to drop them off at the Marble Arch entrance to Hyde

Park. It was just past two when they stepped out of the vehicle.

"We shall walk for a full hour," Adelaide said to the footman.

"Very good, Your Grace," he replied as he reached to raise the step. The two ladies turned and entered the park.

"It will do me good to wander about and see people again," Adelaide said to Charlotte, referring of course to the past two years she had spent in mourning. She did not come to London at all last Season, preferring instead to remain in the country and settle into her new occupancy at the dower house.

"I hope you have not been lonely," Charlotte said, linking her arm through her mother's. "I often look out the window and wonder what you are doing at any given moment. It's strange not having you at the palace. I have missed you."

"I have missed you, too," Adelaide replied, "but it is best for me to reside at the dower house, so that the servants will look to Rebecca for instructions and not come to me. It was important that she take the reins as the new duchess."

"You are right of course. And if you were still living at the palace, they would look to you for the final word on everything, for they love and respect you greatly."

"Thank you, darling. You are kind to say so."

"It is not kindness, it is the truth, and if you ever have any doubts about the running of the household, allow me to assure you that Rebecca is doing an excellent job of it. She had very large shoes to fill, of course, but the servants do respect her. And Lord knows, Devon is happy."

Adelaide smiled. "They have done well, to be sure, and have dutifully provided the dukedom with heirs."

That particular observation made Charlotte laugh, for 'duty' had nothing to do with it. The passion between Devon and his wife had not diminished in the slightest after twelve years of marriage and a nursery full of children. They were a shining example of perfect wedded bliss—as were her other three brothers—Vincent, Blake, and Garrett. It was a happy household, bursting at the seams with the children of the next generation. All was well at Pembroke, and for that Charlotte was grateful.

"And what about you?" Adelaide asked, pulling Charlotte closer to walk side by side on the gravel path. "You are the only one of my beloved children who has not chosen to marry. I know how much pleasure you derive from your writing, but are you happy, darling? Are *you* ever lonely?"

Charlotte felt a pang of discomfort, for she must be lonely indeed, to be driven to take a casual lover. But she couldn't possibly tell her mother that. There were certain things one could not—and should not—say to a parent.

"I am very happy," she assured her mother, and that was no lie. "My writing is fulfilling. I feel blessed to have such a passion in my life. I know that I could never be bored, for there is always a pen and ink jar nearby. Or a book to engage my mind."

"You were always far too bright for your tutors," Adelaide said with a laugh. "What a voracious reader you were, from a very young age."

"I love words," Charlotte replied, "and good stories."

Thankfully her mother left it at that, and did not press her further about loneliness or her looming spinsterhood.

The path began a gradual incline, and Charlotte looked up to see a man walking toward them from the other direction. She recognized him instantly, and her heart swelled with happiness.

William! Her father had come after all—at the very hour she had suggested. Was it possible he had changed his mind?

Quickly she glanced over her shoulder, fearing suddenly that he was here to meet his lady friend, but there was no one behind them.

"Good afternoon!" Adelaide called out, letting go of Charlotte's arm and increasing her pace along the path. She walked ahead to meet him. "What a pleasure to see you, William."

He took hold of her gloved hand, raised it to his lips, and kissed it. "The pleasure is all mine, Your Grace. How are you? It has been almost two years, has it not?"

Charlotte caught up with them. Her father gave her that familiar look of affection, which always made her smile.

"Yes, two years exactly," Adelaide replied. She lowered her voice. "Those were difficult times, as you well know."

She was speaking of the duke's lingering illness and demise and how helpful Dr. Thomas had been through it all.

Charlotte noticed they had not yet let go of each other's hands.

"Have you been well?" he asked.

"Very well, thank you. I have moved into the dower house and the garden there has provided me with many hours of happy distraction. You should see my roses, William."

With a charming smile, he said, "I have no doubt they are exquisite, for you always had a wonderful appreciation for flowers, and such a gift with color."

"As did Theodore," Adelaide replied, out of respect for her late husband.

"Indeed." Dr. Thomas turned to Charlotte. "And how are you on this fine day, my dear? Looking lovely as always."

"Thank you."

"Have you ladies just begun your walk?"

"Yes," Adelaide said. "We arrived only a few minutes ago. Will you join us, William? I would like to hear about your work since we last spoke. Garrett often tells me about your lectures at the university. I am so pleased that you and he have been able to spend so much time together. You have become a tremendous influence in his life. I hope you appreciate how much it means to me."

"It means a great to me as well," he replied as he offered his arm and turned to escort Adelaide down the path in the direction from where he had come.

Charlotte felt suddenly invisible, and wondered if she should tell her mother about William's involvement with another woman. But would that spoil her mother's hopes, if in fact she had any? Perhaps William would tell her of his lady friend today.

Falling back a few steps, Charlotte left them alone to walk together and catch up on old times.

She watched her mother's parasol twirl before her eyes and felt a happy thrill move through her. It had been a most eventful day, full of possibilities. It was hard to believe there was still so much more to come.

Chapter Six

CHARLOTTE WAITED FOR HER mother to retire for the night before she snuck out. It was now almost midnight and she was entering the hotel through the back door as she had been instructed to do. By her lover. Or rather, by the man who would become her lover in the next few hours.

Her belly turned over with a strange mixture of apprehension and eagerness, for she had not been able to erase their morning kiss from her mind. All day she had been reeling with frustrated desire, dreaming about the moment she would feel his hands on her body.

The husky sound of his voice played over in her mind and stimulated her fantasies. She had been distracted from it for only a brief time that afternoon when she had watched her parents walk together in the park and talk for a full hour before Dr. Thomas escorted them back to the barouche.

But that was then, and this was a new moment to embrace. She entered the hotel, closed the door behind her, and found herself in a pitch-dark entryway.

Unable to see her own hand in front of her face, she backed up against the wall and stood very still. Perhaps this had been a mistake. Could she really trust a man she had only just met? What if he had not even come?

Then the floor creaked, a shadow moved in front of her, and she felt the light brush of his lips across her cheek. Her nipples tightened, and her flesh tingled beneath her gown.

"I wasn't sure if you would come," he said in that raunchy voice that singed her mind with erotic images of what would happen over the next few minutes.

"I couldn't possibly stay away," she said. "You have been in my thoughts since the moment we parted."

"The waiting was pure hell."

Then his lips found hers in the darkness and his tongue swept into her mouth with a sexual aggression that roused her senses. She wrapped her arms around his neck and met his kiss with fierce abandon. His hard body trapped her tight up against the wall, while his hand slid down over her hip and hooked under the back of her knee. He lifted her thigh and parted her legs, thrust his hips into hers, and just when she thought he might take her right there in the dark with no foreplay whatsoever, he laid a trail of kisses down the side of her neck and said, "I have a room for us. Join me there now?"

"Lead the way," she replied.

He took her by the hand, and she followed him without question up a narrow staircase lit only by a gaslight sconce at the top. They climbed two flights and emerged into a wide, more brightly lit hallway. Reaching into his breast pocket for a key, he unlocked a door at the far end of the building, and in the very next instant, she was inside the room, kissing him again in the darkness.

He swept her into his arms and carried her to the bed, set her down upon it, and stood over her while shrugging out of his jacket. The light from the city streets outside filtered in through the window and illuminated his broad, muscular chest as he tossed the jacket aside and began to unbutton his waistcoat.

Charlotte leaned up on her elbows to watch the marvelous spectacle of his undressing before her. All of this felt like an impossible fantasy — something she was dreaming about in the late, lonely hours of the night. But it was not a fantasy. This was real. *He* was real, and he was not wasting any time.

"Can I get you anything?" he asked. "A glass of wine?"

If she said 'yes,' would he postpone the ravishment?

"No, I don't need anything," she replied with breathless desire and a heart pounding with excitement.

He removed his waistcoat, tossed that to the floor as well, and proceeded to pull his shirt off over his head. "Would you like to talk first? Some women want to talk."

Curious as to how many women he had pleasured this way, Charlotte shook her head and sucked in a breath at the awesome sight of his upper body, stripped bare. He was a fighter, a sportsman, and she was utterly spellbound by the splendor of his masculine form.

"Before we begin, is there anything at all that you require?" he asked, climbing onto the bed on all fours, like a black panther in the dark.

"I have everything I could possibly desire," she replied.

Reaching out, she cupped his face in her hands, and he came down for another hot, wet, soul-reaching kiss. Charlotte spread her legs wide and wrapped them around his slender hips. She kissed him deeply, thrusting her body freely, without inhibition, for this was a fantasy she intended to live out to the fullest. He was so deliciously enticing and so very male in every way, she thought, as he ran his hands up and down and over her body.

He fisted a hand in the fabric of her skirts and tugged them upwards. In very short order, he found the entrance to her womanhood—that private, sizzling place between her thighs that was at the very heart of her arousal. She writhed with yearning. The wickedness of this encounter intensified the pleasure when his finger slipped into the slick opening of her womanhood.

He stroked her, in and out, while keeping his eyes fixed on hers the entire time. The pleasure of his touch was so intense, all the muscles in her body melted into hot pools of liquid fire. She let out a small moan and then a gasp, while his big hand fondled her.

"You can tell, can't you ...?" she asked.

"Tell what?"

"That I am not a virgin." She wanted to admit it. She wanted him to know he need not be overly gentle.

"Yes."

Her eyes fluttered closed at the flood of erotic sensation. "It's been a long time," she explained, "since I've been with a man." Then his finger slid into her again—slow, deep, and long. "But that's enough talk."

"Not yet," he whispered in her ear. "Tell me what you want first."

That titillating, husky voice swept over her like velvet. "I just want *you*."

It was far too romantic a response, when clearly this was intended to be a casual sexual encounter.

He drew back slightly and looked down at her in the candlelight.

"Was that not specific enough?" she asked, and was strangely relieved when the corner of his mouth curled up in a small grin. "Have I amused you?"

"A little." He removed his hand from her womanhood and swiveled his hips in small circles to rub up against her pelvic bone.

"Perhaps I should have been more specific when posing the question," he said.

She ran her fingertips up and down the smooth corded muscles of his back, then over his firm buttocks. "Ask another, then."

"All right." Still braced above her, he said, "Fast or slow?"

"Both."

"Foreplay? Or straight to the main course?"

"Foreplay, please."

He grinned again. "Naked or partially clothed?"

"Naked."

He paused for a long moment, then swiveled his hips again. "How long can you stay?"

"'Til dawn," she replied. "Not a moment longer."

"Then we have all night." She felt his erection push against her, and every ounce of her being ached to feel his whole body, his bare flesh, hot and damp upon her skin.

"Take this off," he said, running a hand over her bodice, then sitting back on his heels to watch her unfasten the buttons at the front.

She sat up and shrugged out of it, then unhooked the front fastenings on her whalebone corset.

With careful forethought at home, Charlotte had intentionally selected articles of clothing that would not require a maid's—or a gentleman's—assistance. Nothing she wore laced or buttoned at the back.

Tossing the corset carelessly to the floor, she pulled her light cotton chemise over her head, and with breasts bared, leaned back on her elbows to stare up at him.

His gaze roamed from one breast to the other, and she felt her nipples tingle and tighten, as if he had licked them with his tongue.

"Now the skirts," he said. "Take everything off."

Charlotte's body shivered with yearning, for the note of command in his voice was a powerful aphrodisiac all on its own.

Lying back on the pillow, she slowly unfastened the buttons at the side, then untied the ribbon of her petticoat.

"Will you pull it off for me?" she asked, lifting her hips off the bed.

Those big hands slid up her legs and gripped the waistband. Soon her skirts were sliding over her knees and joining the other garments on the floor. The stockings and shoes came off next, and Charlotte marveled at the fact that she felt no modesty, but delighted in the sensation of her nudity beneath the heat of his gaze in the warm glow of the candlelight.

"Now it's your turn," she said, eyeing, with hungry fascination, the large bulge beneath his dark trousers.

He worked the fastenings of his trousers and smoothly slipped out of them as he moved to lie beside her.

Fully naked now, they rolled to face each other. Charlotte reached out to briefly touch her fingertip to his lips. Then he gathered her into his arms, pulled her close, and kissed her passionately for what seemed a perfect, blissful eternity.

Eventually, he rolled on top of her, but never broke the kiss. She spread her legs wide and wrapped them around his hips, while their tongues tangled and danced.

Charlotte sighed breathlessly when he began to move down the length of her body, dropping languorous open-mouthed kisses on her breasts, suckling them for yet another blissful eternity, until she was so overcome with feverish need, her body bucked beneath him.

"Are you growing impatient?" he asked with a sinfully sexy smile that promised something very wicked at the end.

"Intolerably so," she replied, "though it is a frustration I would not choose to forgo."

"You did ask for foreplay," he reminded her.

And he was torturing her with it in the most exquisite way.

"Yes, therefore you should not stop." She smiled and ran her fingers through his thick wavy hair.

With a devilish glint in his eyes, he lowered his head and returned to his task of pleasuring her senseless. He kissed all across and down her flat, quivering belly, past her navel until at last, he arrived at the juncture between her thighs. The kissing—so hot and deliciously erotic—continued down her inner thighs, causing her to tremble and quake. How in the world would she ever survive this?

Then his head moved between her legs and he flicked his tongue over the sensitive bud of her desires, first with quick strokes, then slow, deep velvety ones that made her shudder with an arousal that came from deep inside her womanly core.

She began to breathe faster, moaning with delirious need, but just as the promise of a climax mounted within, he drew back and said, "Not yet."

Wiping his wrist across his mouth, he moved upward, looked down and took hold of his swollen, rigid erection, and placed the thick silky tip at the entrance to her womanhood.

"Are you ready for me?" he asked, and she nodded profusely, feasting her mouth on his, and her hands on the rippled muscles of his shoulders and upper back.

He pushed her legs further apart and slowly slid into her with smooth, relentless mastery, for he stroked all the right places with just the right degree of pressure, as he penetrated her to the hilt.

He withdrew with equal thoroughness, while his hot tongue swirled around hers.

Intensely aroused—barely able to comprehend that she was not floating in the haze of an erotic fantasy—Charlotte cried out with each deep, glorious invasion.

Soon, his slow stokes began to grind harder and faster, and all her muscles turned to jelly. He was hot and heavy above her; his skin was slick with sweat. He grunted like a savage and crushed her mouth with a plunging kiss that stirred her senses into a firestorm of sexual response.

Her climax came quickly, with a sudden intensity she hadn't experienced before. Perhaps it was the sheer thrill of this wicked encounter, or perhaps it was the way he moved. Each stroke of friction was electric, sizzling through her senses and awakening the sexual being which had been lying dormant within her for so many years.

Oh, how she had needed this—this human, physical connection. She had been living such a solitary existence, surrounded only by her books and her family, when what she really needed was a man—a rugged, virile, experienced lover who truly knew how to make love to a woman.

Her body shuddered and convulsed, and when she arched her back, he rose up on one elbow to watch her.

Everything she thought she knew about sexual intercourse was shattered in the explosion of her desires; it was far more visceral, exquisitely more carnal, than any experience from her youthful past.

When the ecstasy reached its peak, then began to recede, and the throbbing of her flesh relaxed, she opened her eyes and looked up at him. Mr. Torrington. *Her lover.*

He was staring down at her with hooded eyes that were full of desire and raging need, while he continued to thrust and pump his hips. Then he shut his eyes, touched his forehead to hers, and grunted as if in excruciating agony as he withdrew from her depths and used his hand to spill his seed onto her stomach to prevent the conception of a child.

She was wildly aroused by the sight of his release. It thrilled her to the very depths of her soul.

He rolled to the side and collapsed beside her like a giant naked sex god.

Had all this truly happened? Part of her wondered if she had been dreaming, for it was everything she had fantasized about in the secret hours of so many lonely nights. No. It was more.

After a moment or two, he turned his head on the pillow to look at her, and while she was struck by how attractive he was—not classically handsome, but extremely charismatic—she had no idea what to say or do next, for this was all so very unfamiliar.

Chapter Seven

*D*RAKE TURNED HIS HEAD on the pillow to look at the woman he had just made love to, and in that moment he wanted to know everything there was to know about her, for she had done something to him just now.

He had come here tonight, fully expecting to have sex with an eager bed partner, and to enjoy it to the fullest—which he had. It was certainly not the first time he had been invited for a night of sexual play with a beautiful woman. Invitations came often from ladies in all levels of Society. Sometimes they wanted it rough. Other times they wanted to be anonymous. But always, they wanted the sort of sexual experience they fantasized about and hadn't achieved with their husbands, for one reason or another.

He didn't know what category Lady Charlotte fell into. She was not a virgin and from what he understood, she was not married. Was she a widow, then? Or simply a modern woman who had chosen to enjoy her freedom?

"Why are you looking at me like that?" she asked with a shy smile that charmed him.

He leaned up on an elbow and studied her face in the candlelight. Her golden hair, splayed out on the pillow all around her, gleamed like spun silk, and her full lips were moist and swollen from kissing him. There had been a lot of kissing.

"I can't help it," he said. "You fascinate me." Not just because she was beautiful. He'd made love to beautiful women before, but Lady Charlotte was different.

"Why?"

He shook his head, for he was bewildered by it himself. "I am curious about you."

The flame on the candle flickered in a draft, and she shivered. Drake reached for the covers and drew them up over her lush, naked form, and covered himself as well.

"That's better," she said, snuggling closer. "Now tell me what you're curious about, sir. I assure you I have no secrets. Not since I told you about my alter ego ... as a man."

He chuckled and cradled her close in his arms, while stroking her hair away from her forehead. "Why are you not married, Charlotte?"

She was a lovely, charming, intelligent woman and the daughter of a duke. She could have almost any man she wanted. What was wrong with the men of England? Were they dense?

"I was engaged once," she said, "many years ago, but he died."

Ah ... "I am sorry to hear that."

"So was I. He was the great love of my young life, and I was devastated by the loss of him. It took me a long time to recover from it, and in some ways, I suppose I still haven't. I never *decided* that I wouldn't marry. At the time, I thought I would eventually find someone, but it never happened. I am not bitter, though. It happened this way because I haven't invited anything different. I am fulfilled by my writing, which keeps my imagination occupied, and I am blessed to be a Sinclair. My family is tightly knit. I have children in my life—nieces and nephews who keep me entertained. So I am never lonely or bored. There is no shortage of activity, or love in my life."

"But the love of a family is not the same as this kind of love." He thrust his pelvis against the curve of her hip and felt a burst of arousal when she wiggled to meet his stroke.

"You're quite right about that," she said with a smile. "Which brings me to ask the same question of you, sir. Why are you not married? You are a desirable man and quite gifted ... *with your hands.*"

He was amused by her coquettish tone.

"I was married once," he told her, surprised that he had not tried to dodge the question. "Like you, it was a long time ago."

"What happened?"

It was not something he ever talked about with women, or anyone else for that matter. At times it seemed like an event that had occurred in someone else's life, not his own.

"She died while carrying our first child," he explained. "She was only a few months into the pregnancy. The doctors said the baby was lodged in the wrong place, not in her womb where it should be. They only discovered that afterwards, when I insisted upon an autopsy. They told me that a tube had burst and she bled to death, from the inside. She was in a great deal of pain in her final hours."

Charlotte laid her hand on his cheek. "I am so sorry. That must have been horrific."

He nodded.

In the years since, he had done his best to forget. It was part of the reason why he left England for America—though not the whole reason. There was so much more he simply could not say.

"When did you learn to box?" she asked, changing the subject, and for that, he was grateful.

"In school. I couldn't have been more than twelve when I threw my first punch in a ring. It was a necessary skill back in those days when we younger boys were bullied by the older ones. I quickly learned to defend myself, however, and the bullying stopped after that."

"I can well imagine, if you hit then like you do now. Did your parents know you were getting into fights?"

"Yes."

"Even your mother? Didn't she try to stop it?"

He scoffed bitterly. "No."

Charlotte's eyes narrowed with curiosity. "Are you and your mother not close? I only ask because of how you shrugged in the boat this morning when I mentioned her."

Drake inhaled so deeply, his ribcage expanded, which caused Charlotte to lean back. "No, we are not close," he said.

"Why?"

For a long while he toyed with Charlotte's long, silky hair, wrapping it around his fingers, then he told her everything she wanted to know. "My father was a drunk," Drake said, "and he beat me on a regular basis until I was big enough to fight back. My mother did nothing to stop that either, and I suppose I have always resented her for it."

"Did you not have any brothers to stand up for you?"

"No, just two younger sisters, but they died of diphtheria, both on the same day, if you can imagine that."

Charlotte regarded him with shock, then spoke with compassion. "I am sorry to hear that."

He shook his head. "It was a long time ago. I was barely twenty. Though I remember their faces so clearly."

He took another deep breath and held her close for a long time. These questions made him feel weary. Thankfully she asked no more after that—though after a while, it appeared she had something else in mind . . .

Drake let his eyes fall closed when she began to lay soft kisses on his chest. He was glad for the distraction. Soon his body warmed with renewed desire. Her lips were soft and moist, her breasts lush and full as they brushed against his torso. A few minutes later he was stiff as a mallet, aroused by the sounds of her breathing, the sensation of her hot lips on his stomach.

She rolled to straddle him, and her long hair fell forward around his face. She kissed him hard, and he reveled in the sultry scent of her skin and hungered for the salty taste of her womanhood.

Cupping her soft fleshy backside in his big hands, he lifted her up and set her down on his raging erection, which lay flat on his stomach. He wanted to plunge himself deep inside, feel her writhe above him with ecstasy, but she slid lightly over him, stroking her slick self on his throbbing length, teasing him into a state of barmy, primitive lust.

He was, quite frankly, surprised that he was ready to go again so quickly after that explosive orgasm, which had left him so thoroughly bushed. But those lips of hers ... those soft breasts that filled his palms so perfectly ... He couldn't resist the desire. His need for her, this very instant, was irrepressible. It took his breath away.

There was no explanation for the intensity of it. They had only just met. Why should she be so different from other women he had taken to bed?

Perhaps because he had revealed so much of himself in a very short time. It was odd, how she understood everything—his boxing, his grief over losing his wife, his need for privacy from the public. In a way it felt as if she were his mirror image in female form.

Bloody hell, he couldn't think about it anymore, for she had taken his shaft in her hand, raised it up, and was now sliding down over him, cloaking him in a slow, hot rush of sensation and passion.

He flipped her over onto her back, and made love to her with everything he had.

ღუჳრ

Drake returned home at dawn, exhausted, for he and Lady Charlotte had stayed up all night. They were like two wild animals in the darkness, desperate to make every moment last, to squeeze the most pleasure out of each stroke, each kiss, each earth-shattering climax.

He was quite certain he had never performed like that before. He had never known himself to be capable of such endurance. With Charlotte, his desires had been insatiable, his strength relentless. Afterward, he had come home to collapse on his bed and had slept for ten hours.

It unnerved him that he wanted her again the very instant he opened his eyes. She was the first thing he thought about, and he wondered what he should do about that. Arrange to see her again? Or try to resist the urge until the desire tapered off—for he felt in danger of becoming obsessed. He had only felt like that once before in his life. Many years ago with Jennie. The frenzy of his passion had driven him to propose in a matter of weeks, because he simply had to have her and possess her in every way. Ten months later, she was dead, and he fell into a hellish vortex of grief that lasted many years. The only place where he could dowse his agony was in the boxing ring. And so ... The Iron Fist was born.

But he had buried that part of himself when he left for America, and the last thing he wanted to do was return to a dangerous passion, which he feared had been awakened last night—in that jewel of a hotel room with Lady Charlotte of Pembroke Palace.

❦

"My word, you slept late today," Adelaide said when Charlotte finally emerged from her bedchamber and walked into the drawing room, where her mother was having tea. "Are you feeling unwell? I was getting worried."

Charlotte sat down on the sofa and picked up a biscuit, for she was famished. "I am fine, Mother. I couldn't sleep last night. That is all. I stayed up reading next to the lamp, which was probably a mistake. My poor eyes."

"You enjoyed it then?" Adelaide asked.

"Oh, yes," Charlotte replied. "Once I started, I couldn't stop." Inside she smiled when she said it.

It was no lie in terms of her immeasurable passions the night before. She still couldn't believe it had really happened. Mr. Torrington was like some sort of god, who had carried her up to a cloud beneath the moon, and there he had pleasured her tirelessly until she couldn't think, speak, or breathe. Her brain had turned to mush, while her body was thoroughly sexed and satisfied. It all felt like a dream today, though she knew it had been real, for she was sore down below and her chin was chafed from the shadow of stubble on his magnificent chiseled jawline. It would no doubt take her a while to recover.

She drank two cups of tea and devoured four biscuits, while her mother updated her about the latest happenings at Pembroke Palace, for Rebecca and Chelsea had both written letters.

Chelsea's youngest daughter Mirabel had caught a frog in the pond and refused to let him go. She had designed a charming rock garden in her toy trunk where he could live. Eventually she had capitulated and set the poor creature free.

Meanwhile, Devon and Rebecca's eldest son—and heir to the dukedom—had been caught kissing a girl behind the stables.

"He's only twelve years old," Charlotte said with feigned shock. "Lord help us when he is old enough to take the curricle into the village on his own. Every young lady within view will swoon in the streets. Poor Devon. He will have his work cut out for him, keeping that boy on the straight and narrow."

Adelaide gave her a look. "He only has what's coming to him, for he was always a charmer himself. I lost a lot of sleep when he was younger."

"Vincent was the worst, though," Charlotte reminded her. "Thank God for Cassandra."

"And June," Adelaide added, referring to the daughter they had conceived out of wedlock. The combination of fatherhood and Cassandra's love had finally convinced Vincent that he was capable of a love that could last a lifetime.

All was well now. All four of the Sinclair brothers were home, happily and respectfully wed. The scandals were forgotten—at least until a new generation of Sinclairs entered the marriage mart. *That* was going to be an interesting time, Charlotte thought.

"Should we take another walk in the park today?" Adelaide suggested. "It was lovely yesterday. How wonderful it was to see William. One should not let so much time pass between visits with old friends."

Old friends . . . But it was so much more than that, surely—for they had loved each other once and were cruelly torn apart. Not unlike Charlotte and Graham, and Mr. Torrington and his wife. At least there was a chance for Adelaide and William to reverse the heartbreaks of the past. They shouldn't squander such an opportunity. William had been resistant the other day, but after seeing her parents together in the park, Charlotte was certain they were destined for each other. William must see it, too, for he had come, hadn't he?

She raised her teacup to her lips and wondered about this other woman he had been seeing. How close were they? How intimate had they become? She set her cup back down in the saucer with a noisy *clink*, for she couldn't bear to think of it.

"Well?" Adelaide said. "Shall we return to the park?

Charlotte placed her cup and saucer on the table and pushed it away. "I would love to, Mother, but before we do, I feel there is something I must tell you. Something about William."

"What is it?" Adelaide asked with a small frown.

Charlotte took a deep breath to get the words out. "He told me the other day that ..." She paused. "That he has been courting someone."

Adelaide sat back. Her expression was unreadable. "I see. Is it serious?"

"I am not certain."

An excruciating moment of silence ensued. Adelaide sat forward again to pour herself another cup of tea. "If he has found someone to care for, then I am very happy for him."

Charlotte struggled to understand what her mother was truly feeling. Was she heartbroken and trying to hide it? Or was she genuinely happy for William?

"Do you still want to go walking in the park today?" Charlotte asked.

"Of course," Adelaide cheerfully replied. "Why wouldn't I? The weather is perfect for it." She took a sip of her tea and reached for the newspaper.

"Then I will summon the carriage." Not yet ready to admit defeat—for Charlotte simply could not accept that William loved any other woman but Adelaide—she stood up and left the room.

ဖွဲ့

After spending his morning on a complex medical case at the hospital, William sat in the window of his private residence in Mayfair, toying with the idea of returning to Hyde Park for a brief walk in the sunshine that afternoon. The exercise would do him good of course, but something aroused his hesitation.

Seeing Adelaide yesterday had been both thrilling and disconcerting, for his heart had come alive at the sight of her under that pretty lace-trimmed parasol. She was past sixty now, but still looked as fresh and youthful as she had when they were young and living in Yorkshire—before he had ventured out into the world to make a man of himself, to earn his own living, and to discover a passion for the field of medicine.

Turning away from the window, he let his gaze fall to his desk—the bottom drawer, in particular, where he kept the letters she had written to him years ago, just before her marriage to the duke, and shortly afterward, when she had written to explain her decision after promising that she would not go through with it.

He had left England upon reading those agonizing words and had vowed never to forgive her. His bitterness had taken on a life of its own, and he had lost many friends. If not for the distraction of his work, he might have ended up a wretched drunkard—or dead from some foolish taproom brawl. Instead, he had traveled to Amsterdam to immerse himself in his training. By the time he returned to England, the fires of his anger had cooled.

Then he had spotted Adelaide, the young Duchess of Pembroke, in a London ballroom, and discovered it was *she* who had become wretched.

He would never forget that night and how his heart had nearly stopped beating at the sight of her. She wore a gown of pale blue silk, and was as dazzling as the sun, just as she had been in the park yesterday. But all was not well, for she had fallen into the very depths of despair. She was miserable and brokenhearted, and had had far too much to drink.

The duke was an unfaithful husband. He was critical of her, and brutally cruel. She had the bruises to prove it.

William had dragged her out of that ballroom onto a moonlit terrace, then down the steps and across a wide lawn to a boat at the river's edge. She was distraught and unable to stop weeping from the sight of him. He had picked up the oars and stolen her away ...

For a week, she had stayed with him in his family's hunting lodge in Cambridgeshire. There, William did nothing but love her. He managed to patch up her emotional wounds and provide her with a respite from her life at Pembroke Palace. They both knew she would have to return eventually, however, for she had three young sons she loved devotedly, and she could not possibly leave them.

And so, at the end of the week, she went home to the duke, and though it broke his heart yet again, William let her go. The duke was relieved to see her. He was so grateful, in fact, that he never raised a hand to her again. Nine months later, she bore twins—Charlotte and Garrett—who showed no resemblance whatsoever to the duke. They were raised at the palace, and it was years before William knew the truth.

Now that the duke was gone, Charlotte and Garrett knew the whole story about their parentage.

Charlotte ... Dear, sweet Charlotte, who desperately wanted happy endings for those she loved. If only she could find her own.

And what about Adelaide? What about her happiness?

Seeing her in the park yesterday had aroused that old familiar ache in William's heart, an ache he thought he had mastered long ago. He laid a hand on his chest and sank into a chair, thought of Dorothea who was so very devoted to him, and finally decided it would perhaps be best to avoid the park that afternoon, for there was simply too much water under the bridge where Adelaide was concerned.

Chapter Eight

A STEADY RAIN FELL HARD over the city of London for the next four days, and there were no further opportunities for walks in the park. Charlotte was disappointed by Dr. Thomas's failure to meet them the day after their initial encounter, for her mother had hinted to him on that day that they would be back at the same time the following afternoon.

"Perhaps there was some emergency at the hospital," Charlotte had said to her as they climbed back into their barouche, after spending two solid hours wandering up and down the paths.

Adelaide made light of it, but Charlotte was vastly disappointed.

A few hours before dinner, she had the copper tub brought to her bedchamber and slipped into a hot bath. While the maid lathered and washed her hair, she continued to wonder what Dr. Thomas was thinking and feeling. Perhaps he had decided, once and for all, that their time had come and gone, and he'd only needed to see Adelaide once to confirm it. She hoped that was not the case, and at the same time, she wondered what her mother truly wanted. Adelaide was not forthcoming about her feelings toward Doctor Thomas. She had never—not once—admitted to still being in love with him. 'We are just friends, nothing more,' she insisted whenever Charlotte broached the subject.

And then, there were Charlotte's own dilemmas about love . . .

No, she reminded herself, it was not love. It was lust that had her body reeling and her mind in an uproar as she lay in the hot bath, breathing in the exotic fragrance of the orange-scented bath oils. How could she help but feel aroused by the sensation of the water lapping over her bare breasts, while the fire crackled noisily in the hearth?

What was Mr. Torrington doing at that very moment? she wondered as she closed her eyes and lay her head back on the rounded rim of the tub. Was he thinking about her at all and yearning for another opportunity to make love?

Her body had not been the same since their incredible night of passion, and it took great strength of will for her to resist the urge to dash over to his house and plead with him to bed her immediately. If only it could be that simple, but she did not wish to become pathetic. She was a mature, intelligent, and rational woman who had lived without a man her entire life. She did not *need* him, and she did not wish to degrade herself by chasing after him like a love-struck puppy.

But was he thinking of her as she was thinking of him? She asked herself that question, and imagined he was as she closed her eyes, slid her fingers over her breasts, slid them lower into the water . . .

১ৼৢৣৣৣৣৣৣৣৣৣৣৣ৽

"Oh. A letter arrived for you while you were in the bath," Adelaide said absentmindedly when Charlotte entered the drawing room shortly before dinner. "I told the footman to leave it with me." She held it out.

"Who is it from?" Charlotte asked as she reached out to take it.

"It doesn't say."

Charlotte turned from her mother and crossed to the fireplace to break the wax seal. She unfolded the letter and read the words:

Tonight. Same place.
—D

A hot thrill exploded in the pit of her belly, and she quickly folded the letter and tossed it into the fire.

"What was that about?" Adelaide asked.

"Just a note from my editor," she replied. "Evidently, they sent another shipment of my books to France."

It was a bald-faced lie, but she was a rather gifted weaver of fiction, hence her literary success.

"That's good news," Adelaide said.

The butler entered the room to announce that dinner was served. As Charlotte rose from her seat to follow her mother into the dining room, she glanced back at the fire, just to make sure no incriminating evidence remained.

❦

When Charlotte arrived at the back entrance of the hotel shortly after midnight, he was there waiting for her. He must have been in the room for some time, for he wore no jacket, only a loose white shirt beneath a dark waistcoat. The shirt was already open at the collar. He had removed his neck cloth as well.

Without speaking a word, he pressed his forefinger to his lips to hush her, took her by the hand and slowly led her up the narrow staircase toward the same room they had occupied previously.

All her senses inflamed beneath the heat of his touch, and the sight of him in the smoky gaslight filled her with sexual yearning. His broad shoulders and narrow hips were perfectly sculpted, and she couldn't help but admire his muscular buttocks as she followed him up the wide corridor. All she wanted to do was tear his clothes from his body and run her hands over every inch of his warm, sinewy flesh. The past four days had been pure agony, not knowing if she would ever see him again, and now her need for him was insatiable.

When they entered the room, he shut the door behind him and locked it. Slowly, lazily, he approached her, while she backed up toward the bed.

He was unshaven tonight, which only added to his rugged appeal and intensified the animal attraction that sizzled her blood. She had never felt such a powerful pull toward any man, and was unnerved by it, but not enough to change her mind about this. She fully intended to enjoy every moment, for as long as it lasted ...

ฅฟฅ

They made love twice, with only a short interval for recovery in between, then fell asleep naked and exhausted while the rain tapped softly against the windowpanes.

When Charlotte woke a few hours later, the bed was empty beside her. She sat up groggily and looked around.

Mr. Torrington was seated in a chair in the corner of the room, watching her. He had pulled on his trousers, but was naked from the waist up. The light from the lamp beside him illuminated his bronzed shoulders and the muscular contours of his chest and arms.

"Good morning," he said in that growling voice that never failed to captivate her.

"What time is it?" She squinted at the darkness outside the window.

"It's almost five, but don't get up yet." He rose from his chair and returned to the bed. Slipping off his trousers, he slid beneath the covers and gathered Charlotte into his arms. She wiggled close and wrapped her leg around his.

"There should be a law," he said, "against beauty like yours."

She gloried at the flattery and pressed a firm kiss to his shoulder. "I feel the same way. Sometimes it hurts just to look at you. I feel like my heart is going to burst. The way I want you … it feels almost criminal."

He brushed his lips across her forehead and stroked her long hair away from her face.

Charlotte closed her eyes and cherished the splendid, beautiful intimacy. Until recently, she had been perfectly content as an unmarried woman. She had always enjoyed her independence and had never felt lonely or deprived of male attention. But after the pleasures of these nights, she realized what she had been missing, and wasn't sure she could face the possibility of never feeling this way again. Never again experiencing the euphoria of the sexual act and all its wonders.

She leaned up on one elbow. "May I ask you a question?"

He nodded.

"What exactly is happening here? I only ask because I need to know if we will do this again. If not ... if it will just be these two nights ... If that is all you want, I will not ask for more. But I must confess—I nearly went mad over the past four days, wanting you as I did, not knowing if I would ever see you again."

His expression was inscrutable as he lay on his back, looking up at her. "Why didn't you pay a call? Or send me a note?"

"I didn't know if you wanted me to."

"So you waited for me to make the next move."

"Yes."

He laid his hand on her cheek and stroked softly with his thumb. "Come closer," he whispered. "Lie down."

She laid her cheek on his shoulder while he ran the pad of his finger up and down her arm. "You were in my thoughts as well," he said. "Every day, especially at night."

Her heart turned over in her chest. "Then why did you wait so long to send a note?"

He took his time answering. "I was trying to fight my desires. I wasn't comfortable with how ... overwhelming they were."

"That, sir, I understand completely, for I, too, was fighting my feelings. I don't wish to become overpowered by them."

For a long moment, they lay together in silence until Charlotte was forced to ask her question again.

"So, what should I expect, Mr. Torrington? Are we to be regular lovers? Or will we part ways and continue to do battle with our passions?"

"First of all," he said, "you must call me Drake, at least in bed." He continued to rub the rough pad of his finger over her shoulder, and she wanted to disappear forever into the magic of those hands.

"And yes," he continued, "we are to be regular lovers, for there is no need to torture ourselves. Are you in agreement?"

"Most definitely," she replied, leaning up on her elbow again.

She was feeling far too exuberant at the thought of more nights like this, and perhaps other sorts of activities as well. She longed to be near him, to be able to admire him, even from a distance, and to flirt with him ... touch him.

"I must have your word, however," he said, "about something."

"Anything."

"You will not tell anyone about us, and you will not expect me to accompany you to the theater or other public places. I am here for the summer only, Charlotte, and not for the Season. I will not welcome a slew of invitations. I do not want my presence here to become known, nor do I wish to become a source of gossip."

"Because you were notorious once," she said, understanding him completely, "and you wish to lead a private life. As do I. So I will ask the same of you. Please do not reveal my secret to anyone. I am referring to what you know of Victor Edwards, of course."

He kissed the top of her head. "Agreed."

She smiled and hugged him close.

"I am not sure how long I can continue to sneak out in the middle of the night, however, without getting caught," she said. "Are there any other places, other times, we can meet?"

"How about a long, leisurely drive in my coach?" he said. "Or another boat ride on the Thames?"

"Or a picnic in the woods," she suggested, "if this infernal rain ever stops."

He ran his thumb lightly across her lips. "Secret lovers, then," he said.

"Yes, but just to be clear, I will not be your love slave. You may not wish to fraternize with London Society, but I do not wish to become a recluse either. I have a life you know, and there are always invitations to balls and whatnot. So do not be surprised if sometimes I am not available at your beck and call."

"Understood," he replied, looking amused.

"Excellent. On that note ..." She tossed the covers aside and swung her legs over the edge of the bed. "I must go before the sun comes up."

"Not yet." He leaned across and reached out to massage her shoulder. "Ten more minutes ..."

Intrigued, she glanced back at him. "I know what you have in mind, sir, and ten minutes is not nearly enough."

"Anything is possible, darling, when passion is involved. Now lie back down, and I promise I will make it worth your while."

Naturally, Charlotte surrendered, for it was an offer she simply could not refuse.

Chapter Nine

*T*HE HALLOWAY BALL WAS an absolute crush the following night. Everyone who was anyone was in attendance, for the Prince of Wales had announced he would be there to enjoy the famous Halloway turtle soup.

The ballroom, located on the second floor of the fashionable Mayfair mansion, was marvelously illuminated by four crystal chandeliers that reflected the light from hundreds of candles and a number of shiny brass sconces on the walls.

As Charlotte entered the ballroom with Adelaide, they were greeted by their hosts. Once inside, they helped themselves to glasses of champagne, brought around by a handsome liveried footman, and spoke to many acquaintances, old and new.

Charlotte was invited to dance a quadrille within ten minutes of their arrival, and Adelaide was escorted to a half circle of chairs with an excellent view of the floor, where some of her oldest, dearest friends had staked their territory.

It was the Earl of Whitcomb who first invited Charlotte to dance. He was a friendly and handsome older gentleman with four grown children, and had been widowed just over a year ago. He was often the object of speculation, for he had his heirs. Now all he needed was a pretty young wife on his arm to make his life complete. Charlotte had always rubbed along well with him, but considered him a friend, nothing more.

The fact that she was not attracted to him in that way was doubly obvious tonight, after experiencing the throes of true passion in the arms of a man who excited her beyond comprehension. As she danced through the steps, she found herself wishing that Mr. Torrington was not so against making appearances in Society, for it would have made her night more than special if she could see him here and dance with him. Perhaps to escape onto the balcony alone with him, and secretly flirt as passionate lovers.

But he would not be here tonight, or any other night for that matter, so she vowed not to let that spoil her mood. She would dance as much as she liked, and she would enjoy herself.

When the set came to an end, Lord Whitcomb escorted her back to her mother, and in that moment she spotted a familiar face and felt her heart leap with joy. The earl bowed politely and took his leave, and Charlotte tugged at her mother's sleeve.

"Look who is here," she said, gesturing toward the small cluster of guests on the far side of the room, nearer to the orchestra. "It's Doctor Thomas."

"Oh yes," her mother replied. "He lives here in Mayfair. Of course he would be here."

He was kissing the gloved hand of another lady, however, and escorting her onto the floor.

A heavy lump of disappointment dropped into Charlotte's belly. She glanced at her mother, who was also watching.

"He is always so popular," Adelaide said, without the slightest display of 'woe is me.' "You can hardly blame the ladies, can you?" she added. "He is such a handsome and amiable man."

Charlotte studied her mother's countenance. Sometimes she was not certain how Adelaide truly felt about him. Perhaps she *did* consider him a friend and nothing more.

As Charlotte watched him dance, she wondered if his partner could be the woman he had spoken about in his office. The one he had been courting.

She was younger than he was, perhaps in her late forties, and was blessed with a slender figure and strikingly dark features. They made a handsome couple and spoke to each other as if they were very well acquainted.

A short while later, however, Charlotte saw him escort another lady onto the floor. She was equally lovely, and he was equally charming.

Then there was a third lady, at which time Charlotte decided to give up keeping count.

Truth be told, she was angry with him. Surely he knew she and Adelaide were in attendance. Charlotte had been out on the floor a few times, yet he had not come over to say 'hello.'

"Why won't he at least acknowledge us?" Charlotte whispered in her mother's ear when they had a moment to themselves.

"Who in the world are you referring to?" Adelaide asked with some displeasure as she sipped her champagne.

"Doctor Thomas, of course. He has danced with every pretty lady within ten paces of his person since the moment he arrived."

"You sound jealous," Adelaide said with a laugh. Then she leaned very close to Charlotte. "Darling, you must forget about this and not imagine that we will ever go back to what we once were. How many times must I say it? We are friends now, and that is all we will ever be."

Charlotte suddenly felt very foolish with her lofty dreams of romantic destiny and clever matchmaking. But how could she simply let it go? She knew everything about their broken hearts all those years ago. They were like Romeo and Juliet. For once, Charlotte wanted that story to have a happy ending. She wanted to fix the past. To rewrite it, if she could.

Just then, someone spoke her name. "Lady Charlotte, I wonder if you would do me the honor of joining me for the next set?"

Managing a courteous smile, she set down her glass and laid her gloved hand upon the gentleman's arm. "How kind of you to ask, Mr. Tremont. I would be delighted."

She followed him onto the floor.

ଚୁ୧ଧ

As Charlotte began the first steps of another quadrille, Adelaide set down her glass and turned toward the large bank of French doors at the rear of the ballroom, for they opened onto a wide flagstone balcony lit by torches at each corner. There were few people outside, for a fine mist hung in the air. It was the sort of weather that could cause a lady's hair to frizz instantly and give her a chill. Adelaide could not care less about her hair, and she was so angry, a good shiver in the cold might serve her well.

She was angry with Charlotte for pushing her toward William—as if she were some young debutante experiencing her first London Season, and was on the hunt for a handsome gentleman with whom to begin a thrilling courtship.

Adelaide was hardly a young girl, and she'd had enough life experience to understand her own heart and manage her life. She had been married for over forty years and had given birth to five children. She had survived that tumultuous marriage, and somehow, in the end, had made a success of it. Then she had nursed her husband through a long and devastating illness in the final decade of his life. She had stood by him faithfully and devotedly.

She had suffered a great deal of heartache and tragedy in her younger years, yet she felt blessed with what she had achieved, for she had five wonderful children and a house full of grandchildren. If given the choice, she would not change a thing about the past, for it would alter the present, and she firmly believed she had lived the life she was meant to live.

"Adelaide ...?"

She was standing at the cement balustrade looking up at the dark, cloudy night sky, when the sound of her name, spoken so familiarly, caused her to jump. She turned around to see William standing in the doorway, looking as handsome as he had over forty years ago, when he had come home from Italy to try and convince her not to go through with her wedding.

"You must be freezing out here," he said, removing his jacket and approaching her with it. He draped it over her shoulders. It was still warm with the heat and musk from his body, and it felt ... heavenly.

"Thank you," she said, hugging it about her. "I was just beginning to shiver."

"What are you doing out here?" he asked. "I was frustrated just now, for I wanted to dance with you. Unless your card is full? Am I too late?"

She looked up at him in the flickering torchlight. He was not wearing his spectacles this evening and looked not a day older than ... Oh, what did it matter? He would always be the same young man she had known since girlhood. His eyes, his smile, the sound of his voice ... They would always be the same.

"Charlotte tells me you have a lady in your life now," she said, for she and William knew each other well enough to be honest and open, and it would not do her any good to pretend she was not aware of it.

"Yes," he replied, as he moved to sit upon the balustrade. "I have been courting someone."

"I am so happy for you," she said. "I hope she is everything you deserve, and you deserve the very best, William. Will I get to meet her one day?"

He gave no reply, and instead turned to look out over the dark lawn. "It was such a pleasure to see you in the park earlier in the week," he said. "I'm sorry I did not return the following day when you said you would be there."

She waved a dismissive hand through the air. "Please, do not worry yourself. I know how busy you are."

He met her gaze again, and she was unnerved by the fluttery response of her heart.

But how could she not be amazed by him, by his friendship especially, when it had survived so many challenges? He had been a loyal, devoted presence in her life—so helpful, and most importantly, so forgiving. She was not sure she could have behaved as he did if the roles had been reversed and he had married another.

"It wasn't that," he said. "I was not so busy, but I wasn't sure it would be wise, for I had a previous engagement that evening—to escort my lady friend to the opera. I feared my head would be spinning in circles."

"How so?" Adelaide asked, though she already knew the answer. He did not wish to stir up painful memories of the past.

After all I put him through, I cannot blame him.

She sighed heavily and pulled his coat tighter about her shoulders.

"Charlotte is playing matchmaker, you know," she said with a light tone that overturned any proper social distance between them.

He chuckled. "Yes, I know. She came to my office last week and tried to casually suggest that we meet at the theater. And at the park the next day."

"Oh, my dear girl. She never told me that. What did you say to her?"

"I told her that she should mind her own business."

Adelaide smiled. "Well done, William. And yet you came to the park regardless. You are just encouraging her, you know."

He nodded in agreement, and she was intensely aware of his hands curling and flexing around the edge of the balustrade rail he sat upon.

"Why *did* you come to the park?" she daringly asked.

He rose to his full height and turned to look out at the darkness beyond the lawn. "Because I wanted to see you," he said. "You know how deeply I care for you, Adelaide. I needed to see your face and assure myself that you were well."

"I appreciate your concern," she said, "but my happiness is not your responsibility."

"I know that," he said, "but I will always need to know how you are." The orchestra began a waltz, and he turned to look back at the ballroom. "Will you dance with me?"

She, too, watched the swirling array of light and colorful gowns as couples swept past the open doors. Then she removed his jacket from her shoulders and handed it back to him. "I would be delighted."

He smiled and slipped his arms into the sleeves, then gallantly escorted her inside.

ᘛᘚ

When Charlotte woke the following morning, she was torn between feelings of happiness and frustration. She wanted to shout joyfully from the rooftops, for she had watched her mother enter the ballroom on Dr. Thomas's arm and waltz with him after a lengthy conversation alone on the balcony. At the same time, she was confused, for he had danced with every other woman in the room before making his way to speak to her mother.

Charlotte's emotions were a mixed bundle indeed, for she had gone to bed dreaming of Mr. Torrington and wishing that he had been at the ball as well, so that she could have waltzed with him the entire night, instead of dancing with countless other partners who did not stir her blood the way he did.

By noon she was starving for a mere taste of him, the smallest glance, even from a distance. So when the footman delivered a letter to her shortly after luncheon, she snatched it from the silver salver and tore it open in a matter of seconds, reading it in its entirety before looking up to dismiss the young man.

> *This afternoon. Torrington House, 2pm. Come*
> *around to the stables at the back.*
> *—D*

The stables? Did he wish to go riding with her? In public?

Erring on the side of caution, she donned her black riding habit with the silver buttons, her fashionable new boots, which had been polished to a fine sheen since the last time she wore them, and brought along her riding crop as well.

At precisely two in the afternoon, she alighted from the family coach in front of Mr. Torrington's London residence and instructed her driver to return for her in one hour, and to wait on the street.

The vehicle pulled away from the curb and she watched it reach a fair distance before she ventured around to the back of the house. She crossed a small gravel courtyard, taking note of the fact that there was no one about—no grooms or other servants from the household—and the stable door was slightly ajar. She could hear an odd pounding noise from within.

Pulling the door open with her leather-gloved hand, she peered inside.

The stable was empty. There was no carriage in the center corridor, or any horses in the stalls, yet she could still hear the repetitive sound of hard pounding.

Quietly she walked toward the back and found the source of the racket. It was Mr. Torrington and his iron fists. He was moving about in the last stall, punching a large leather sack full of sand or some other heavy substance, which was secured with a rope and suspended from one of the rafters above.

Charlotte stood for a moment watching him, until he circled around and noticed her standing there.

He was crouched slightly at the knees in a defensive stance with both fists wrapped up in white gauze. When their eyes met, he straightened and laid a hand on the bag to stop it from swinging. Her body flared with sexual awareness at the sight of him, for he wore a pair of tight pale gray breeches, black boots with laces, and nothing else. His bare chest and arms glistened with shiny drops of sweat, and Charlotte could almost feel the fierceness of his attitude as fighter.

She said nothing while he caught his breath. Then slowly she moved closer until she could lay a hand on the giant leather bag. "I think you killed it."

Without cracking a smile, he wiped a forearm across his sweaty brow and spit off to the side.

Charlotte inclined her head at him, feeling suddenly as if she were not welcome there. "You sent me a note," she reminded him. "It's two o'clock. Here I am."

He exhaled sharply. "Yes."

He began to unwrap the gauze from his hands and tossed it carelessly onto the floor, which was swept clean of straw. An old rug had been laid out to cover the plank floor.

The sight of his naked chest and the smell of his sweaty body were not things a lady should be presented with—yet she was fascinated and aroused by both. "Are you practicing for something?" she asked.

"Not practicing. This is a punching bag. I prefer it because it doesn't bruise or bleed, and it doesn't punch back."

"A definite advantage," she replied. "You could go all day with it."

He approached her, slung a hand around to the small of her back, pulled her hips tight up against his own, and planted a hard, salty kiss on her mouth.

By the time he was finished devouring her like a midday meal and released his grip on her body, she was breathless with delight and could have fainted right there.

"I'm glad you came," he said. "Dressed for a good gallop, I see."

She should have been shocked by the wicked innuendo, but to the contrary she was thrilled by the implications, for they were lovers now. She was surprisingly at ease with the open sexuality that pulsed like a steady heartbeat between them.

"You said to meet you in the stables," she explained. "I was raised in the country, sir, and learned at a very young age that an invitation to such a place usually involves a saddle and stirrups."

He took her riding crop from her, tossed it aside, then removed her top hat and hung it on a nearby rung.

"Will you be disappointed if there is no horseflesh involved?" he asked.

"That depends."

"On what?"

"On whether or not you can lock that stable door."

Drake's eyes narrowed in on her with devilish intent, and while he strode to the door, she began to undo the buttons of her bodice. She was shrugging out of it by the time he returned, and hung it on a second rung next to the one where he had placed her hat. Now she stood before him in her heavy riding skirt, corset, and white cotton chemise.

She moved slowly around the punching bag, circling it to stay just beyond his reach. Eyes fixed on the other with feverish desire, they ran their hands over the smooth worn leather.

"What does it feel like to punch a man in the ring?" she asked.

"In a bare-knuckled fight," he replied, "it bloody well hurts."

"Hurts you or him?" she inquired further.

"Both of us, I suppose."

"Then what, may I ask, is the appeal?"

He continued to circle around the bag, his eyes hungry for sex, while she moved in the opposite direction. "A question I've often asked myself over the years," he replied. "Was it the cheering crowd? The triumph when the other man fell at my feet? Or the buckets of money?"

"How big a fortune did you win?" she boldly asked.

"Enough to buy my passage to America and purchase holdings in three different railroads once I got there."

"Very impressive." She ran her fingers over the smooth brown leather and looked up at the rope that was slung over the beam. It creaked like an old ship whenever the bag swung back and forth. "How much does this weigh?"

"Forty pounds, I imagine."

"That's heavy."

His eyes narrowed with amusement. "Are you teasing me, Lady Charlotte?"

"I don't know. Am I?"

He stopped his circling and stared at her. "I reckon you are. A tease, I mean."

Her pulse thrummed with excitement. "Clearly I am a very naughty lady. What are you going to do about it?"

His mouth curved up in a devilish grin, and he shoved the punching bag aside. The next thing she knew, it was swinging back and forth across the width of the stall and she was pinned up against the back wall, while his big hand slid over the curve of her hip. She turned her head to the side to allow him full access to the sensitive flesh at her throat, which he kissed hungrily, sending a flood of tingling arousal into her core.

Good Lord ... She could barely comprehend the grandeur of his muscular shoulders and back as she ran her fingers over the muscles, still slick with his sweat. Then his mouth found hers and he kissed her roughly, sweeping his tongue inside while his hands tugged her skirts upward and he worked at the fastenings of his breeches.

Seconds later, he was plunging his thick, rigid length into her, and she gasped with pleasure at that most welcome invasion. Last night she had dreamed of this after her return from the ball. While memories of the music played in her head, she had imagined Mr. Torrington's hands on her body, and had trembled with pleasure at the mere thought of being taken by him, just like this—roughly and quickly, without foreplay, up against a wall. It was all so expected, yet so very shocking to her lady-like sensibilities. What had become of her?

She was not a wanton harlot, yet she felt like one whenever she thought about this man or fell shamelessly into his arms. She cared for nothing but the hedonistic pleasure of his embrace, the masterful stroke of his hands, and the sumptuous flavor of his flesh upon her lips and tongue.

He pumped into her hard and fast, shoving her up against the stable wall while she gasped with every glorious thrust.

Then a climax rose up within her and her vaginal muscles clenched tight and convulsed repeatedly around the driving force of his manhood.

She was still crying out when he shoved deep and hard, almost painfully into her depths, and grunted like a tortured beast in a cage.

Suddenly weakened, he pulled out of her. Her skirts fell to the floor while she fought to regain her sanity. He backed away and fastened his breeches, then sat down on the rug. Legs stretched out, he leaned on both arms and looked up at her in amazement. "Christ ... I meant to pull out sooner. I don't know what happened."

Charlotte decided to join him on the floor to recover. "Neither do I. That was wild. But I think it's a fairly safe time." Her courses were due soon, but one could never be sure. She was surprised he had taken that chance.

For a long time they sat in a silent haze of shock and sensual fulfillment.

"Did you attend the ball last night?" he asked, out of the blue.

"Yes. It was very enjoyable."

"Did you dance?"

"Quite a bit, actually."

He stared at her. "How many times?"

Charlotte frowned at him, for she could sense his displeasure at the image of her swirling around the floor in the arms of countless other men. "I couldn't tell you the exact number—I would have to consult my dance card—but I saw no reason to refuse any invitations. The music was lively and the room was festive. It was a crush, but a most excellent crowd."

He continued to stare at her, then flopped onto this back, bent his knees, and looked up at the rafters. He reached out and pushed the bottom of the punching bag. It swung back and forth across the stall.

"I was in a foul mood last night," he said, "knowing you were there, doing Lord knows what with God knows whom."

"I was *dancing*." She wiped at the perspiration at the back of her neck. "You could have come, you know. I would have secured you an invitation, then we could have danced together. I would have enjoyed that."

He sat up again. "I told you, I don't go to balls. Not in London."

"Then why are you asking me about it, as if I had been disloyal by going without you?"

She stood up and brushed the dust off her skirts, then went to fetch her bodice from the hook on the wall. She pushed her arms into the sleeves and was fastening the buttons when Drake stood up as well and came to assist her.

"Let me do that," he said.

She stood in silence while he took over the task. Looking up at his face, she studied the details of his many scars and wondered what he was thinking.

"You didn't *want* to come to the ball," she reminded him."Yet you seem annoyed with me. Are you jealous?"

His blue eyes lifted. "Jealous? Yes. I want to thrash every man who put his hands on you."

She smiled at that. "Then you should come next time and put on a show. The Prince and his Marlborough Set would love a scandal like that. Fisticuffs in a ballroom. They would talk of nothing else for weeks."

Drake fastened the last button at the bottom and turned away from her.

"You are not laughing," she said. "I was only joking."

"I told you I want no part of the social Season."

"But you want to be with me," she clarified.

"Yes. Privately."

"And then what?" She watched him move to a table in the corner, pour a glass of water from a tin pitcher, and guzzle it. "You will return to America and we will never see each other again?"

He turned to face her, wiped at his mouth, and tilted his head to the side. "*Charlotte . . .*"

She scoffed at what she took to be a patronizing tone. "What . . .? Am I not permitted to imagine that you might wish to accompany me somewhere interesting? A museum perhaps. Or would we have to wear hooded cloaks and masks?"

His eyebrows pulled together in a frown. "What is wrong? You knew the rules when we entered into this."

She made a fist and gently punched the leather bag. "Of course I knew the rules. You were very clear about them. I am simply frustrated, I suppose. It was not such a perfect night at the Halloway ball."

"How so?"

She moved to the wall, leaned back against it, and crossed her booted legs at the ankles. "I was missing you, for one thing, and none of the gentlemen could distract me from thoughts of you. On top of that, one particular gentleman, who I believe is destined to marry my mother, danced with every other lady in the room before saying the smallest hello to her. He eventually danced with her, but it felt as if his actions conveyed a message to remind her that she has no claim on him. I was hurt and angry."

"You speak as if it were *your* heart at stake, not your mother's. How does she feel about it?"

"Oh, her feathers are never ruffled," Charlotte replied. "She insists they are just friends."

"Maybe they are."

Charlotte shook her head dismissively. "No, that cannot be so. He was her first love, and she almost didn't go through with her own wedding because she couldn't bear to leave him behind. They were desperately in love, but were torn apart like Romeo and Juliet. Now my mother is a widow and he is also free. He never married, in fact, which I believe is a testament to his undying love for her. She is out of mourning now, and I believe with all my heart that she deserves to live out the rest of her days with the man she never stopped loving."

"I am sure she deserves every happiness," Drake said, "but it sounds to me as if you are playing matchmaker and might want to consider minding your own business."

Charlotte was taken aback. "I only want my mother to be happy."

"But perhaps another marriage is not what *she* wants," he said. "They are adults now, not children. I am sure she knows her own heart."

"I don't agree with that at all," Charlotte argued.

"Which part?" he said with a laugh, as if she were a fool.

Charlotte gaped at him. "I assure you, I know my mother better than you do, and I am positively certain that she is lying about her feelings. She loves him with every inch of her being, and always has, but she is too proud or perhaps too frightened to admit it."

"Why does she need to admit it?" Drake asked. "If they love each other, it will happen on its own. They shouldn't require *you* to act as their guide. It is not up to you to force people to love."

Charlotte crossed the stall to fetch her hat and riding crop. "I don't know why I brought it up. Perhaps I am too much of a romantic, while you are, quite clearly, the opposite."

She placed her hat back on her head, tucked in a few errant wisps of hair, then pulled on her gloves. "I must go. I told my driver to return in an hour. He will be out front by now."

"I will walk you out," Drake said as he pulled on his shirt, then his waistcoat.

Charlotte turned to leave before he was fully dressed, and he was still buttoning the waistcoat when he hurried to follow her across the gravel courtyard.

"When will I see you again?" he asked just before they reached the front of the house.

"I am not sure. I have some things to do this week. I may keep my Victor Edwards identity a secret, Drake, but I still have a social life, and it is very full."

She stopped beside the coach, and the footman hopped down from the box to lower the step. "Good day, Mr. Torrington," she said.

"Good day," he replied, just before the footman helped her inside and shut the door.

Chapter Ten

W*OMEN*.
 Drake ran a hand through his hair as he watched the coach pull away from the curb. Lady Charlotte did not look back, and he wondered what the devil he had been thinking back there in the stables. He'd actually admitted to being jealous that she danced with other men. And that wasn't all.

He should have kept his big mouth shut about her matchmaking schemes instead of openly criticizing her and shining a light on the fact that he had no romantic inclinations whatsoever. He had effectively reminded her that this was a temporary sexual affair, and there was no danger of his heart becoming involved because that was not what he wanted.

However, that particular assertion caused him some distress there on the sidewalk as he watched the coach grow distant—for he was completely flustered and angry with himself. Should he go after her and apologize? Would that smooth things over?

Hell, he knew better than to argue with women over matters of the heart. It was a losing battle every time. Hands on his hips, he paced back and forth for a moment, then tried to sweep the argument from his mind as he climbed the front steps. He entered the house through the front door, but stopped in the entryway when he locked eyes with his mother, who appeared out of the parlor.

"Who was that woman just now?" she asked, looking displeased.

"No one," he replied, and started for the stairs.

"Wait. I want to speak with you."

He paused with one hand on the newel post. "What about?"

His mother cleared her throat. "Come into the parlor where we can speak privately."

With a heavy exhale, he followed her into the front room and watched her close the door behind him.

"Sit down," she said, uncorking the decanter and pouring him a glass of brandy.

He accepted the drink, but said, "I prefer to stand."

"Fine." She moved to the sofa and sat down. "I saw you just now, leaving the stables, half dressed."

"I was training." She knew he kept a punching bag in one of the stalls.

"With a woman?"

He eyed her intently, took a sip of the brandy, and grimaced as it slid hotly down his throat. "That is not your concern." Then he realized it was the second time in twenty minutes he had spoken similar words to a woman.

"To the contrary," his mother replied, "it is very much my concern when you are carrying on a torrid affair with the daughter of a duke. Don't look at me like that, as if I have been spying on you. The Pembroke crest was more than visible, emblazoned on the side of her coach for all the world to see. It was parked out front for quite some time. It was Lady Charlotte, was it not? The woman who required your assistance after her purse was stolen? Oh yes, I know who she is. She is an attractive woman, the sort you've always admired—tall, blond—but she is not for you, Drake. Surely you know that."

"I know no such thing." He finished his drink and irritably set it down.

"Don't be a fool. You are only here for the summer, and you are not part of her world. Besides, she is a spinster, as I am sure you are aware, and I daresay she is clinging to her respectability by a mere thread."

"How so?"

"She is far too independent, for one thing. They say she has her own income. That she *earns* it. From *writing*."

So it was not such a well-kept secret after all, he realized, and wondered if Charlotte knew she was the subject of gossip.

Damn London Society and all its aggravating flapping tongues. Did people have nothing better to do? There were certain social circles in America where things were no different, especially in New York and Newport, but the majority of plain folk were too busy working their way up in the world to be bothered with such frivolity.

"I don't give a damn if she has her own income," Drake said. "In fact, I respect her for it, and so should you. She does not rely on a man for her happiness. She is intelligent and self-sufficient."

His mother rolled her shoulders haughtily. "I see. Do you intend to marry her then?"

He scoffed. "Did you not hear a word I just said? She is independent. She is not seeking a husband."

"Ah, there it is then," his mother said. "The improper nature of your acquaintance, just as I suspected. It is a secret, and no doubt torrid, affair."

He shook his head in disbelief.

"I just don't understand how this could have happened," she continued. "You have remained hidden from the world since you arrived, like some sort of night creature."

He took a moment to still his temper. "I didn't come home to socialize," he told her, "and I thought we discussed this already and put an end to it. I am here to settle our financial affairs and see that your future is secured. I have a life in America and I will be returning to it as soon as possible. Other than that, how I live my life while I am here does not concern you."

His turned and strode from the room.

"What about Lady Charlotte?" his mother asked, rising to her feet. "Is she aware that you will be leaving?"

He paused in the doorway. "Yes, she understands, so there is no danger of heartbreak, if that is what worries you." Though he doubted that was the problem.

"Wait! Please, Drake. It is an improper affair. You *must* break it off."

Drake frowned and turned to face her. "Why does it even matter to you? Nothing else about my life has ever mattered before."

She squinted irately. "You forget that I am always left to mop up the scandals you leave behind. It will be *my* reputation that is tarnished if word of this gets out."

"It won't," he firmly told her as he walked to the stairs, suspecting that the affair was already over, for Charlotte had left on a very bad note.

ᖫ৻৶ᖰ

Charlotte stepped out of the coach, entered her house, and handed over her hat, gloves, and riding crop to the butler who greeted her at the door.

"Brandy, Lady Charlotte?" he asked, for he understood her moods, and though he never spoke a word otherwise, or asked any intrusive questions, he somehow took one look at her and knew when to bring tea and when to bring brandy.

"Yes, thank you. To my boudoir, if you please."

"Right away, my lady."

A few minutes later, she flopped onto her bed and covered her face with her hands.

What is wrong with me? Why did I walk out on him like that?

Sitting up, she removed all her hairpins, ran her fingers through her hair, and shook everything out to cascade freely down her back.

A knock sounded at her door, and her maid arrived with a drink tray. "Would you like me to brush out your hair, Lady Charlotte?" she asked as she set the tray on a table and poured the amber liquid into a glass. "Or prepare a bath before dinner?"

"No thank you, Mary. I would prefer to rest awhile."

"Very good, milady," she said. "I'll close the drapes and make sure you are not disturbed."

"You are an angel." Charlotte waited patiently for her maid to leave before she moved to the chair by the window and went over every ridiculous thing she had said to Mr. Torrington before she walked out of his stables.

Or perhaps it had not been ridiculous. Perhaps it was an unconscious act of self-preservation—to spoil everything now and protect herself from what might transpire if she continued with this affair. Perhaps she *wanted* to sabotage it.

It had all seemed so exciting when she made the decision to enjoy Mr. Torrington as a lover, seemingly without any consequences, for he would soon be gone. Eventually it would all seem like a dream, as if it had never really occurred.

But there was a risk of pregnancy, and she was well acquainted with how such an accident could ruin a person socially. Her brother Vincent had taken a mistress, and together they had borne an illegitimate child. The scandal was so monstrous, they'd been forced to leave the country, and it was ten years before they returned.

And Vincent had *married* Cassandra. Charlotte wasn't sure that Mr. Torrington would propose marriage in such a case.

Perhaps it was better this way, she told herself. He would think her a romantic fool who had bitten off more than she could chew, and he would refrain from sending any more scandalous invitations. Clearly she was not cut out for reckless affairs. She gave too much thought to it, and it was quite obvious that she was becoming infatuated. *More* than infatuated. She couldn't get the blasted man out of her mind. A less rational woman might confuse such feelings with love and begin to dream of a happily ever after.

But she was not one of those women. She knew the difference between reality and fantasy. Love and lust.

Charlotte tipped her head back against the chair and stared up at the ceiling for a long while. She imagined Mr. Torrington riding up to the house, calling out to her from the street, and getting down on his knees when she came to the window—to beg her to continue their affair.

Good God.

Charlotte lifted her head. She *was* one of those women. This proved it, and so did the matchmaking, and her dreams of dancing with Mr. Torrington at a glittering ball. Heaven help her, she did want something more than lust and basic carnal sex. She was completely besotted, and if she weren't careful, he would become the source of another romantic tragedy in her life. This time of her own making. For she feared she was falling fast toward love. She yearned for permanence and confidence in his regard, for him to want to be with her forever ...

Alas. That wish was not to be.

She sighed and finished her brandy, thankful at least for this opportunity for private and personal reflection, so that she would not continue to behave like such a hopeless romantic.

ბღჳყბ

Five days passed, during which time Charlotte and Adelaide, respectively, heard nothing from Mr. Torrington or Dr. Thomas. Charlotte was soon convinced that she had spoiled everything and frightened Drake off when she spouted her romantic ideals in the stable. She could hardly blame him, but wished overwhelmingly that she could go back to that moment and agree with him. Admit that she had meddled in her mother's private affairs and that life was not a fairy tale. Could never be.

It was quite possible that the path of one's life could shift and take on a new direction. Perhaps there was someone else in her mother's future, and her own as well. Perhaps Mr. Torrington had merely been a necessary experience to teach her that lesson and remind her she was not past her prime. She was still a passionate and attractive woman with a full heart, who could love and be loved. Perhaps she had needed to discover that she deserved more than a temporary physical affair. She was a soulful person and wanted something deeper than that.

Why was it that she was always looking for the reasons *why* life unfolded the way it did? Couldn't she simply accept things the way they were, and not question the *why*?

❦

It was on the fifth night, after she and Adelaide returned home from the theater, that Charlotte found a letter waiting for her on her pillow. Wondering who had placed it there, she picked it up and broke the seal.

> Lady Charlotte,
> Please do me the great honor of joining
> me on the river at dawn tomorrow. I wish
> to apologize for my lack of understanding
> the other day, and my insensitivity to your
> wishes. I will wait outside your door at 6:00.
> If you do not wish to see me, I will move on
> at 6:15 and refrain from ever contacting
> you again. Though I confess, it will pain me
> greatly to keep that promise.
>
> Sincerely,
> D

Charlotte closed her eyes and pressed the letter to her breast, while joy flooded her heart. She had never been so happy to read any letter in her life.

How odd, that when she had finally convinced herself that her relationship with Mr. Torrington was completely sordid, as well as over, this letter arrived and spoke of something else. Was this only a ruse to seduce her into more lovemaking? Or had his heart become involved too?

She longed desperately to know the answer, and could hardly wait until the morning.

Chapter Eleven

*H*E HAD TRIED. TRULY he had. Drake had considered the risks of a summer affair with Lady Charlotte—the beautiful, passionate, romantic daughter of a duke—and for five days straight, had fought against the urge to contact her. In the end, he could bear it no longer. The thought of not spending the full summer with her drove him mad with frustration. He decided it would be best to let this affair run its course. Sometimes what was forbidden became coveted, and what he really hoped for was an enjoyable affair that would end amiably for both of them. They would part as friends, feeling satisfied with the time they had spent together, and remember each other fondly.

He was not yet sure if that were possible, for he sensed, with the high emotion, this could turn out to be the very worst sort of passionate and turbulent relationship—the kind that ended in tears and hatred. It was possible that Charlotte could show her true colors very soon and become the sort of woman he avoided—possessive, demanding, and jealous. But none of that mattered now, for he was not yet ready to give her up.

Though he *had* tried.

It was nearly 6:15 am when the front door of Pembroke House opened and she walked down the steps.

His relief was immense, and his pulse raced at the sight of her in that formfitting, pine-green walking dress and attractive straw bonnet.

He slid across the seat and opened the door for her. She climbed inside and sat beside him, her body turned at a slight angle toward him while she removed her gloves.

"I was surprised to receive your invitation," she said, laying her gloves on her lap. "I thought perhaps we were through. After the way I behaved the other day ..."

"The way *you* behaved?" He shook his head to object. "You did nothing wrong. It was I who was unreasonable. I dismissed your feelings and passed judgement when I knew few details about the situation. I cannot blame you for walking out on me—and I am sorry."

Her cheeks flushed with color and her eyes glistened with happiness. "Thank you, but no apology is necessary. I am just so glad you invited me to join you this morning. I missed you."

The words were tender and sentimental, and he was both touched and unnerved by them. "I missed you, too." *Had he really just said that?*

The next thing he knew, he was leaning close and pressing his mouth to hers, holding her tight as the coach rumbled over the city cobblestones and his body drummed with desire.

"I don't want to fight with you," she said breathlessly, sitting back. "You are here for such a short time. Part of me wants to make the most of it and be happy and smiling all the time, but another part of me knows that would be superficial, and I don't want that either."

"Nor do I." *What the blazes had he just said?*

"I understand," she continued, "if you don't want to venture out into Society, and I can hardly blame you. All the foolish gossip drives me mad sometimes, so I will not press you to escort me anywhere. I will be happy to proceed as we initially intended, and see each other only in private."

"I am happy to hear it, Charlotte."

He clasped her hand in his, and neither of them said anything more for the duration of the drive.

ତଙ୍କୃଚ

It was humid and warm that morning, so Charlotte decided to leave her bonnet and gloves in the coach.

While Drake stepped into the boat and untied the ropes on the jetty, she looked back at the land they had just driven across. "Whose property is this?" she asked.

"It belongs to an old sparring partner," Drake replied. "He lets me keep my boat here."

"That is kind. Have you seen him much since you arrived?"

"A few times." He reached out a hand to her. "Come now."

With his assistance, she stepped into the boat, which rocked back and forth, bobbing wildly against the jetty until she sat down.

Drake took his position, his back to the bow, and picked up the oars. Soon they were cutting fast through the calm water with Drake's powerful thrusts of the oars. Charlotte felt wonderfully alive.

She knew enough not to try and make conversation with him while he worked so strenuously against the current, so she distracted herself by sitting back against the transom and looking up at the morning sky.

Fifteen minutes later, Drake lifted the oars out of the water and let out a deep exhale. "That was good," he said.

"Did you come every day this week, even when it was raining?"

"Yes," he replied, breathing heavily. "I like rowing in the rain. It keeps me cool."

They were in a wide, lazy part of the river and floated idly for a few minutes, drifting downstream slowly while ducks quacked close to the shore.

"This feels like home to me," she said. "The peacefulness reminds me of Pembroke. I enjoy the city, but I prefer the country. Tell me about your life in America, Drake. Do you live in the country or the city?"

"I have two homes," he said. "One is in the city of Boston, and the other is on a stretch of land called Cape Cod. It's a picturesque seaside community. I enjoy the salty air and the roar of the surf."

"It sounds lovely."

"Let me know if you ever decide to make a transatlantic crossing," he said. "I would enjoy having you as my guest."

Charlotte smiled. "I will remember that. Thank you."

She watched him dip one oar into the water to use as a rudder, while he stroked with the other to turn them around.

"I want to tell you something," she said, feeling rather reckless suddenly with the urge to open up.

"There is a reason why I am so passionate about my mother's romantic life. I am not just bored and seeking amusement. I want her to be happy, of course, but I want these two particular people to be together because ..."

She hesitated, for this was an intimate family secret. She wasn't sure why she wanted to reveal it, or why she felt Drake should know. Would he even care? She wasn't certain, but everything in her heart and soul screamed at her to reveal this to him.

"I want them to be together because they are my true parents."

Drake's eyes lifted, and he raised the oars out of the water so that they floated to a stop again. "I beg your pardon?"

"The gentleman I am attempting to pair up with my mother is my real father. So obviously, he was more than her first love. He was also her lover for a brief time while she was married ... when things were unbearable for her at the palace."

"How exactly were they unbearable?"

Charlotte explained how the duke was unfaithful, abusive, and cruel in the early years of their marriage, probably because he had realized his wife's heart secretly belonged to another. She also explained how her mother had almost run off and abandoned her role as Duchess of Pembroke.

"She changed her mind at the last minute," Charlotte told him, "for she knew the duke would never let her see her sons again if she left him."

"Your brothers."

"Yes. Devon, Vincent and Blake. Garrett is my twin and we are both illegitimate. But no one knows it, so I must ask you not to betray my confidence."

He laid a hand over his heart. "You have my word of honor."

"I hope that helps you to understand why I was upset over what happened at the ball. It's more complicated than I initially let on."

"I see." He lowered the oars back into the water, leaned forward, and gave a firm stroke to pick up some speed. "Was the duke a good father to you?"

She shrugged. "He was always kind to me, but I suspect that was because I was the only girl. He was harder on Garrett, because he knew we weren't his, and there was the issue of the succession. If anything had happened to the three older ones, Garrett could have inherited the title. But our father preferred to keep my mother's infidelity a secret, because he felt it reflected poorly on him as a husband."

"I am sorry to hear all of that."

"It wasn't so bad in the end. After mother came home to him, he realized how he had driven her away, and he turned over a new leaf. He spent less time in London, more time in the country with her. I believe they grew to love each other. But that is all in the past now. He passed away two years ago."

"My condolences."

Charlotte leaned over the side to drag a finger through the water as they skimmed along its clear surface.

"Since we are sharing secrets," Drake said, "I have one, too."

She pulled her hand from the water, shook off the droplets, and sat forward. "What is it?"

He glanced over his shoulder as he rowed smoothly back toward the jetty. "The reason I left England twelve years ago was to escape something I did."

She was forced to wait an unbearable number of seconds before he continued.

Then at last he said, "I punched a man so hard that I killed him instantly. And it didn't happen in the ring."

Chapter Twelve

CHARLOTTE GRIPPED THE SIDES of the boat and fought to keep the evidence of her shock to a minimum. Drake—her perfect fantasy lover—had killed a man?

Swallowing uneasily, she said, "There was a mystery surrounding your disappearance when you left. Was it because of this? Did anyone know what happened?"

"Very few people. One close friend whom I trusted with my life—the man who owns this property. He was my trainer. My mother knew as well, and Mrs. March, the housekeeper."

"Why did you leave?" Charlotte asked. "Was there a warrant out for your arrest?"

Was it murder? She was curious, but couldn't bring herself to ask such a question.

"They questioned me at the time," he explained, "and it was deemed an accidental death. No charges were laid. I believe my connections as nephew to Earl Lidstone played a part in that, though I certainly didn't try to use them. My mother did, however, which buried the scandal, but also deepened the rift between us, because I didn't want her help. I specifically asked her to stay out of it."

"You felt you should have paid a price for what you did?" Charlotte asked, "even though it was deemed accidental?"

"The definition of accidental can be murky sometimes."

Charlotte tilted her head to the side. She studied his expression in the early morning light and wanted very much to understand him better. "What exactly did happen?"

He continued to row steadily to recover their position, while every muscle strained with the long strokes. "I was drunk one night after a prize fight, and had pockets full of coin to spend. I was mixing with a seedy bunch back then and making my way through Whitechapel when I heard a man and a woman shouting at each other.

"I looked up at a veranda on a second floor where the man was shoving the woman around. She had a baby in her arms. I climbed up on a barrel and somehow found myself on the landing. There were two smaller children inside the flat, hiding under a table, trembling and looking terrified. The woman had obviously taken a few beatings already. Other than that, I don't remember much. The details are foggy, but I do recall how I loathed that man for not cherishing what he had—a wife and children—while I had lost mine.

"He may have swung a punch at me. I don't know. So I cannot say whether it was self-defence or not. All I know is that I hit him and killed him, right there in front of his children. Then his wife nearly scratched my eyes out. 'He may have been a brute,' she said to me, 'but he brought home a good wage from the dockyards.' I gave her all the money I had in my pockets that night, then gave her more afterwards when no charges were laid. I still send her money to this day, all the way from America. And I will continue to do so."

"But clearly it was accidental," Charlotte said. "You were only trying to help."

He shrugged. "Perhaps. All I know is that when I heard the baby cry in the mother's arms, all I could think of was Jennie and how it wasn't fair. It was pure rage that night. But it forced me, from that day on, to learn to take my rage out on a bag of sand, instead of other men."

"Except for the day you rescued my purse from that thief."

"He's lucky to be alive," Drake said. "It was a good reminder."

"Of what?"

"That I have no control when my blood boils."

Charlotte squinted as she gazed across the water. "I am sorry that happened," she said with compassion, "but I don't see why it should keep you from mixing in Society. It was a long time ago and from the sound of it, it was an accident. You have nothing to be ashamed of, Drake, and as you said, the scandal was buried. No one knows about it."

"I appreciate that," he said, "but I have no interest in stuffy drawing rooms and the idle lifestyles of the English aristocracy. I've been in America too long. This is no longer my world, and I have no interest in being dragged back into it."

"Then you must do what you feel is right," she said. "Follow your heart."

His eyes narrowed with resolve as he began to row toward the shore. "Follow my heart? That sounds far too romantic for an ex-prize fighter like me."

"I don't think so," she replied, watching the riverbank grow nearer. "Where are you taking us? The jetty is still half a mile away."

"I don't want to go back yet," he said, looking her over with heated appreciation. "For the moment, I want to heed your advice, and follow my heart."

The hull of the boat scraped along the gravel riverbed and gently bumped the grassy bank. It was an isolated location beneath a giant weeping willow that gracefully dipped its branches into the water. Charlotte knew exactly what he had in mind as soon as he lifted the oars into the boat and leaped onto the bank.

He held out his hand. "Care to take a walk through the woods with me?"

She made her way to the bow and, with his help, climbed out. "How deep do you intend to take me?"

"Deep enough to continue this conversation in private."

"As if the river were not private enough?" she replied with a playful note of sarcasm as she followed him into the greenery.

࿔ळ෴

They made love slowly and tenderly that morning, hidden away beneath the shelter of another large willow tree not far from where they'd left the boat. For Charlotte, it felt less like a sexual fantasy for the purpose of physical gratification, and more like an act of love, though she did not allow herself to believe that too wholeheartedly. Just because something was tender and romantic did not mean it was more than what it was—a temporary summer romance that would end before the autumn breezes began to blow.

In the coach, during the brief journey back to Pembroke House, she sat with her head on Drake's shoulder while he held her snugly in his arms. They traveled in a companionable silence that filled her with a sense of well-being and contentment.

"I understand," she said, "why you do not wish to join Society here in London and I would not dream of pushing you into it. But would you consider coming to Pembroke Palace for a few days to enjoy the solitude there? I must warn you, of course, that it will not be *completely* quiet. I have a large family and there are many children about. There is a great deal of lively conversation at dinner, but we are an intimate group and very tightly knit. You might enjoy yourself. Do you like to fish?"

"I do," he replied, stroking a finger across her shoulder.

She lifted her face to look up at him. "Then why not come? You might enjoy it. There is laughter and entertainment, yet no gossip ever leaves the palace. The Sinclairs are a loyal bunch, and if I bring you as my guest, you will find yourself most welcome."

"I don't know," he said with a frown. "I didn't come home to become involved with people."

Pleased that he used the word *home*, she sat back and laid a hand on his cheek. "Whether you will admit it or not, you have already become involved with *me*, Drake, so unless you want to change your mind and quit this affair, why not simply make the most of it? Come to Pembroke and fish and row on our lake. Come riding with me in the afternoons, and then you can have me to your heart's content at night."

"*Have* you? That sounds rather wicked, Lady Charlotte. Won't your brother, the duke, have something to say about that?"

"He won't know, for I will introduce you to one of the great secrets of Pembroke Palace, and I am not referring to the scandals, past or present. I am referring to secret passageways. A number of rooms are connected with false walls and hidden doorways. If you are very good, I will show you the subterranean passages beneath the chapel as well, which are said to be haunted. Then I will tell you about the Pembroke Palace curse, which forced all four of my brothers to marry hastily over a decade ago, in order to save their inheritances."

"Sounds intriguing."

"It is. Will you come? I promise it will be very different from London."

He considered it for a long moment. "What will your brothers think of me?"

"Do you play billiards?" she asked.

"It has been a while, but yes."

"Then you will fit right in. Please come."

It was at that moment they drove into Mayfair and pulled to a stop in front of Pembroke House. He appeared reluctant to let her go.

"All right," he said. "I will."

Feeling blissfully happy, Charlotte kissed him on the cheek and quickly slipped out of the coach before he had a chance to change his mind.

Chapter Thirteen

*A*N UNEXPECTED SENSE OF inevitability washed over
Adelaide as she rose from her bed and took a
seat at her desk. She had been tossing and turning for
the past hour, but knew that she must do something
to ease her mind. She picked up her pen and dipped it
into the ink ...

Dear William,
It has been nearly a week since we last
spoke at the Halloway Ball. I want to thank
you again for the delightful dance, and
for the generous loan of your coat on the
balcony.

I am writing, however, to tell you
something wonderful about Charlotte. It
seems at last that a gentleman has won
her affections. As you well know, it has
been many years since she has opened her
heart to love, so I am hopeful this may be a
turning point.

She is, as always, mindful of gossip
and has asked me to refrain from speaking
of their acquaintance to anyone outside
of the family. But I consider you to be

family, so I do not believe I am betraying
any confidences by writing to you now.
I will, however, at Charlotte's request,
keep the gentleman's identity a secret, for
reasons I cannot go into here. I am just so
very pleased that she has finally taken an
interest in someone.

In that regard, I will be leaving London
and returning to Pembroke Palace tomorrow,
as we have invited the young man to join
us for a few days in the country. No doubt
Devon and the boys will be keen to 'evaluate'
him.

I speak in jest, of course. If Charlotte
adores him, so shall the rest of us, for her
happiness is what matters most, and she
has certainly earned it. In the meantime, I
will do my best to play matchmaker. Wish
me luck.

Now I must bid you farewell, for I am not
sure when I will return to London. Perhaps
not for a while.
Take care of yourself,
Adelaide

ॐ

Dear Duchess,
Thank you for keeping me abreast of
Charlotte's news. I will be thinking of you
all and hoping for a happy outcome. And
there is no need to thank me for our dance
at the Halloway Ball. It is I who must thank
you for the pleasure of your company.
Sometimes it feels as if not a single day has

passed since our friendship in Yorkshire.
It is hard to believe we are easing into our
autumn years, when at times I feel like a
much younger man with my whole life yet
ahead of me. There is still so much I wish to
see and do. So many answers I still seek in
the field of science and medicine, and I have
not yet been to America. I would like to see
the Grand Canyon. Do you know of it? Now,
with railroads and steamships, it is not an
impossible dream.

Your letter today was a balm to my
soul. How wonderful to be a witness to
your devotion as a mother. Your children
are truly blessed, as are all the people of
Pembroke, to have had you as their duchess.

Please forgive me if I cannot write more
than this tonight. I lost a patient today at
the hospital, and I am feeling low.

Please write to me from Pembroke and
keep me informed about Charlotte and her
young man. It cheers my heart.

—W

Dear William,

We arrived at Pembroke last night. I am
so sorry to hear about the patient you
lost. I often think about the challenges of
your profession and I am always moved
by your strength and heroism. I saw it for
myself when Theodore was ill. You were an
invaluable source of support and comfort to
all of us, and there are no words to convey
the depth of our appreciation. I don't know
much about the patient you lost, but if he

or she had a family, I am sure they were grateful for your kind care ...

And now permit me to cheer your heart and write about Charlotte. I am beside myself with joy, for I have not seen such passion in her since all those years ago, when she first met and fell in love with Graham.

To be honest, I believed a part of her had died with Graham and their unborn child, but now everything seems new to her again. She was positively radiant on the train when she told me about her new gentleman. They seem like kindred spirits, and I feel that fate has played a hand in bringing them together.

Perhaps I sound like a romantic fool, but I cannot help myself. My heart is bursting with hope. I have always longed for Charlotte to be happy, as I am sure you understand, for I know how you have wanted the same. Cross your fingers, William, that a broken heart can one day be mended.

—Adelaide

❧

Back in London, William read Adelaide's last letter three times before he placed it carefully in the drawer with all the others ... and locked everything away.

Chapter Fourteen

MR. TORRINGTON WAS DUE to arrive on the five o'clock train from London. A coach had already been sent to fetch him, and Charlotte could not seem to relax. It had been five days since she went rowing with him on the Thames. She had not seen or spoken to him since, but he had been in her thoughts to an alarming degree. At times she was completely swept away by a flood of happiness and anticipation, for she could not wait to be alone with him again—to touch him, and be touched by him. She wanted to show him the estate and introduce him to all the members of her family—her brothers and sisters-in-law, all her nieces and nephews. She wanted to enjoy the country setting with him, and most importantly, she looked forward to pleasurable and discreet lovemaking at night.

Other times, however, she was concerned by the intensity of her emotions, for this wicked affair had obviously gone beyond the physical. All the evidence was there. She longed for him constantly and dreamed that he would change his mind about returning to America. Last night she even imagined what she would say if he told her he could not live without her, begged her to become his bride and cross the Atlantic with him. Would she accept? Would she become a married woman, leave her home for a new life in a world she knew nothing about?

Clearly her heart—in all its jagged, broken places—had become deeply involved, for she was dreaming of her own happily ever after and feared everyone knew it.

Charlotte jumped when her sister-in-law entered the drawing room and said, "He should be here at any moment. Are you ready?"

Charlotte turned from the window and laid a hand over her heart. "Oh, Anne. You frightened me."

"I do apologize," Anne replied. "It was not my intention." She moved a little closer. "We are all very much looking forward to meeting Mr. Torrington."

"I know, and I appreciate your support."

Anne watched her for a moment. "Something is wrong," Anne said. "I can see it in your eyes. You seemed so happy yesterday, but now it's as if the sun has moved behind a cloud. Have you changed your mind about him?"

Everyone knew how Charlotte had met Mr. Torrington—how he had rescued her from peril at the hands of a purse thief. Anne also knew that Charlotte had gone rowing with him twice at dawn, but no one knew the true nature of their affair, that it had already gone well beyond the limits of what could be considered proper. It was unequivocally scandalous.

Charlotte remained at the window. "No, I have not changed my mind, and that is the problem. He is only here for the summer, and I have known that all along. I was determined to guard my heart and maintain an emotional distance, but it seems I have fallen head first into an ocean of romantic dreams. I cannot stop thinking about him, and I am afraid that ..." *Of what am I afraid, exactly?*

Charlotte asked herself that question over and over.

Had she, despite all her best intentions, fallen in love?

"He is not my type at all," she argued. "Wait until you see him. He is rough and reticent. Never cheerful. When he speaks, his voice is very gruff." Yet to her it was like soft black velvet across her skin. "Perhaps you and the rest of the family won't like him at all. I don't know why I do. I really shouldn't."

Anne smiled sympathetically. "We will like him perfectly well, for he came to your rescue when you were in danger, and for that we are grateful. As for the rest of it, the only thing that matters is that you are happy. If he makes you happy then enjoy yourself over the next few days. The rest will sort itself out."

"Will it? Because I fear I may become very unhappy indeed when September rolls around and I am forced to give him up. Oh, Anne. Perhaps I shouldn't have been so cavalier about all this. I truly believed I could manage it, but clearly I have a very sensitive heart."

Anne's gaze was drawn to the window. "Well, you are going to have to batten down the hatches, my dear, for the coach is on its way up the drive."

Charlotte, too, looked out, and all her senses came alive with excitement. He was here. *At last.* Heaven help her, he was like some sort of sizzling-hot addiction she could not resist ...

༺ღༀ

Drake leaned forward in the seat to look out the coach window. There it was ... Pembroke Palace.

God above. What the blazes had he been thinking when he accepted Lady Charlotte's invitation to come and enjoy a few days of solitude in the country? She had mentioned fishing and lovemaking, but this was no cozy retreat. The palace was a monstrous bastion, the home of an exalted duke and his entire family. Never mind that it was situated at the top of a steep hill, lording over the entire county like a powerful monarch, surrounded by ancient oak trees and stringently manicured gardens.

Drake grew tense at the mere sight of the place and was half tempted to tell the coachman to turn around, for he had made a mistake. He didn't belong here. He wanted to leave. The only thing that kept him from doing so was the agony of a relentless desire that grew more intense with every revolution of the coach wheels. Over the past few days, without Charlotte, he had slipped into a pathetic state of sexual obsession.

The coach passed under a giant triumphal arch and rumbled across a cobbled courtyard toward a wide set of steps at the front entrance. There was a flurry of activity as groomsmen came running. A number of servants spilled out of the palace and quickly lined up under the portico and clock tower.

Then he spotted Charlotte, like a beacon in the night. She was dressed in a formfitting blue and white striped afternoon dress, and she practically floated down the steps like an angel with wings. Behind her, members of her family followed, and Drake wondered which man was her brother, the duke.

God help him. What was he doing here? This was not for him. Yet desire had prodded, and he'd not possessed the will to stay away.

Eventually the coach pulled to a halt and a footman opened the door. Charlotte was the first to greet him.

"Mr. Torrington, welcome to Pembroke."

Drake fought not to let his gaze linger too long on her full pink lips or her luscious bosom, for there were others approaching.

Charlotte made all the introductions—first to her eldest brother Devon and his wife, Rebecca, the duke and duchess. Devon was a tall man with dark features, while the duchess was an attractive woman with flame-red hair.

Next, he met Lord and Lady Vincent. These were the two who had chosen to leave England after a desperately scandalous situation. Cassandra had been Vincent's secret mistress while he was engaged to another, but he'd jilted the fiancée in order to marry Cassandra after she'd borne him an illegitimate child. According to Charlotte, their daughter June was so charming and beautiful at twelve years of age, that everyone who came in contact with her was so bedazzled, they were blind to the fact that she had been born out of wedlock.

Lastly, he met Lord Blake and his wife Chelsea, a handsome, amiable couple, and Anne, who was married to Charlotte's twin brother, Lord Garrett. Garrett, a surgeon in London, was unable to join them that particular week.

Everyone was pleasant and welcoming, but Drake was pleased to begin the march up the steps with Lady Charlotte on his arm, for all he wanted to do was determine the place and the exact moment he could make love to her.

ତଦ୍ଧତ

Not ten minutes after he was shown to his room to settle in and change for dinner, Drake heard a creaking sound, like weak floorboards in an old, broken down country house.

He recalled the stories Charlotte had told him about the palace—that it had been built on the ruins of an ancient monastery destroyed during the reign of King Henry VIII. According to legend, the subterranean passages beneath the foundations were haunted by the souls of the dead monks.

Charlotte told him she had lived here all of her life, and her only terrors had come at the hands of her brothers, who, as children, enjoyed frightening their younger sister. She also mentioned a few unfortunate incidents with her father, the duke, in his final years when he suffered from mad delusions, and carried on conversations—with one ghost in particular.

None of it was real, of course, yet for some reason, all the little hairs on Drake's arms stood on end when the ominous sound of the creaking floorboards grew nearer, like footsteps approaching, yet he knew he was alone in the room.

His gaze shot to the drapes as they wafted suddenly on a draft, as if someone had opened the window, but he could see it remained shut tight.

Drake moved to the desk, picked up a heavy brass candlestick holder, backed up against the wall, and wielded it over his head. "Who's there?"

The tapestry beside the bed fluttered. Drake strode toward it and wrenched it back. He nearly lost his head when Charlotte appeared, as if she had passed like mist through the wall.

"You can put the candlestick holder down now," she said with a laugh as she pulled a secret door shut behind her and let the tapestry fall back into place. "You looked as if you were about to brain me with it."

With a sigh of relief, he set it down. "I thought you were a dead monk," he said.

Charlotte smiled at him, and her warmth was more radiant than the sun. He wanted her instantly, ravenously.

"Do you not remember what I told you about the secret passages?" she asked. "Not all the rooms have them, but I made sure you were put in one of the good ones."

Her hair was like spun gold in the early evening light streaming in through the window, and like Eve, she stood before him, the embodiment of temptation. He knew then that it had indeed been a mistake to come here, for clearly he was losing control of this affair, he but it was too late to turn back now, for he wanted her with a raging desire that was unmatched in its intensity.

"I hope you don't mind that I snuck in so soon," Charlotte said alluringly as she approached. "But I couldn't wait until later. It feels as if I have been waiting for days. I tried, but another minute without you seemed unbearable. I needed to see you. Touch you. Feel your hands on me."

Passion blazed through his senses so forcefully, that he found himself tearing at his neck cloth with one hand while simultaneously cupping the back of her head with the other. He pulled her close.

The kiss was hard and rough and when their tongues met, a savage lust pounded through his brain and filled him with urgent discontent, for he was tired of fighting this. He wanted to surrender to it, to enjoy her body and her tender affections without any thought for the future.

The curve of her hips was somehow hypnotic as his hands searched and stroked around to her sweet bottom.

"Take me to the bed," she breathlessly pleaded, and he swept her into his arms, carried her a few short steps, set her down, and quickly unbuttoned his waistcoat. Seconds later he had ridded himself of the garment and was tugging his shirt off over his head in a mad rush to feel her luscious body against his bare skin.

He ached with need. It was a brutal yearning that reminded him of days gone by, when he had yielded eagerly to his violent side. But this was something else. He didn't want to pillage or destroy. All he wanted was to possess.

The next few moments were a frenzy of desperate gasps, as if they were both drowning in their sexual appetites.

"Is the door locked?" Charlotte asked as he came down naked upon her, about to penetrate.

"No," he replied, though perhaps he should have lied.

"Pray God no one walks in," she replied, and that was enough. It was all he needed—permission to plunge into her with all the savage intensity that had exploded like a bomb inside his brain over the past few days, ever since their lovemaking under the willow tree by the river.

He drove into her smoothly and pleasurably, and she clung to him with unbridled passion, as if he were her salvation. In that moment, he felt transformed, like a man without sin or shame. His body trembled against exquisite sensation as he continued to work in and out of her hot, slick depths, his mind unaware of the physical world beyond the friction and slide of her lush body. He made a sound of deep, primal satisfaction that caused her to moan softly in response, like an echo.

Their passions grew together to a fevered pitch, and their orgasms came in a matched rhythm that seared his soul. He convulsed above her, clutching at her bottom, pushing into her as deep as he possibly could while she thrust her hips forward and whispered in his ear, "Drake ..."

Moments later, they lay weak, sated, and happy, clinging to each other like two lost souls.

"I missed you so much," she said, and the words aroused him anew.

"I missed you, too," he replied. "Nothing was the same. All I did was count the minutes until I could see you again."

Oh God, had he really said that aloud? Had he let down his guard completely? He—the undefeated boxing champion of England—was surely down for the count, blinking up at the ceiling in a foggy haze of semi-consciousness.

But he wasn't about to let go. He hugged Charlotte as tight as he could without crushing her, and reveled in the sensation of her legs entwined with his.

He was still inside her, drowning in sweet bliss and the liquid heat of her juices mixed with his own. It was the second time he had taken such a risk by neglecting to withdraw before he climaxed. The fact that he was not concerned about that was a miracle in itself, for if they conceived a child, he would have no choice but to marry her. Despite what some might say, he was a man of honor.

But it was more than that. Perhaps a part of him wanted to face such a future. Her pregnancy, though dangerous, could tie them together forever and not permit him to leave her behind. *But a pregnancy?* No one knew better than Drake the risks of such a condition.

Charlotte shifted beneath him and he felt her delicate ribcage expand. Recognizing the effort it took for her to breathe with his weight upon her, he carefully rolled to the side.

Charlotte reached down to pull the coverlet up over their naked bodies, then curled into him. He wrapped an arm around her. She rested her head on his shoulder.

"This is the room where my mother stayed the night before her wedding to the duke," Charlotte said. "Remember when I told you that she almost didn't go through with it?"

He nodded.

"Well, that was not nearly half the story," Charlotte continued, "for she actually planned to run off with her young man. He came into this very room from behind the tapestry, just as I did tonight, and they tried to leave together to make their way through the tunnels. Her father caught them before they could flee, however, and dragged my mother back after beating the young man to a pulp. She went through with the wedding only to protect her love, because her father threatened to kill him otherwise."

"Good Lord," Drake said. "How barbaric."

"I agree."

"Did you know your grandfather?"

"No, he died before I was born."

Drake stroked Charlotte's bare shoulder and kissed her on the forehead. "Was your mother very miserable in her marriage?"

"At first, yes, but she says they eventually grew to care for each other. The duke mellowed in his old age."

He sighed. "Well, from what I gather the dowager duchess seems like a lovely person. She deserves happiness. I hope she finds it."

"I hope you find it, too." Charlotte lifted her head to look up at him.

"Who says I haven't?" he replied without smiling, for that very serious confession was unplanned and left him reeling. He felt caught in a vortex, spinning and spinning, deeper and deeper into passion. Now that he was here at Pembroke, he didn't want to spend a single moment away from Charlotte. He wanted to make the very most of it.

Perhaps they both simply needed to take their fill before summer's end, and then they would part as friends. But when her lips touched his, something swelled inside of him, and he felt a deep connection to her, one he knew could last a lifetime, if given a chance.

He thought of how she must have mourned the death of her fiancé and unborn child, just as he had mourned the death of his wife and child. Charlotte had not gone on to marry another; neither had he. Now she wanted her mother to be happy and settled, which was the same reason he had come home—to ensure that his own mother was taken care of. So many things the same ...

He kissed Charlotte tenderly in the twilight and was very glad he had not told the coachman to turn around. It didn't matter that she lived in a palace, nor would it have mattered if she lived in a hovel. He desired her, and he simply had to have her.

"I'm so glad you came," she said with a smile.

"So am I." He kissed her again, but she pulled away and slipped out of his bed.

"Where are you going?" He didn't want her to leave.

"It's time to dress for dinner," she said. "I need to sneak out of here before someone catches us."

He lay back on the pillow, tossed his arms up behind his head, watched her don her chemise and petticoat. "What would your brother do if he did catch us?" Drake asked. "Give me a good thrashing, I suppose."

"Heaven help him if he tried. He'd end up unconscious on the ground. He wouldn't even know what hit him."

She bent to pick up her corset and fastened the hooks in the front, then pulled on her skirt.

"Maybe he'd bring out a shotgun and force me against my will to marry you."

Charlotte picked up a pillow and pitched it at him. With lightning fast reflexes, Drake caught it in front of his face.

"Maybe he'd have to hold a shotgun to *my* head, to force me to marry *you*."

She was laughing as she said it, but Drake suddenly found himself leaning up on an elbow, studying her expression. "Is that what it would take? Or would you surrender to me willingly?"

Her expression grew serious, then she turned to pick up her bodice. "I don't know," she said, pushing her arms into the sleeves. He wished he could see her face. "I never liked hypothetical questions."

It was better than a 'no,' he thought.

Feeling rather satisfied, he lay back down on the pillow to watch her fasten the buttons up her front. She had turned around at last, then leaned over the bed and kissed him quickly on the mouth. "I have to go now. Otherwise we might find ourselves facing shotguns—*un*hypothetically."

"If you would stay ten more minutes," he said, "I guarantee it would be completely worth it."

She gave him a mischievous smirk, then circled around the bed and disappeared behind the tapestry, leaving him alone to ponder his life.

ᘯᘓᘔ

With a burst of excitement, Charlotte left Drake's room, entered the dark passageway and picked up the candle she had left in one of the wall sconces. Had he really just said those things to her? Was he only teasing, or did he mean it? Would he welcome a shotgun wedding?

Would she?

Why was she so inconceivably happy at the thought of it? How ridiculous!

It was not a proposal, and even if it were, she was not sure she would want to marry him. She must maintain control of her intellect and not become swept away by the magic of his kiss and the pleasure of his hands on her body. For all she knew, he could make a terrible husband, and she certainly did not want to live like a recluse.

No, she mustn't become swept away.

But she *would* enjoy this. She would enjoy the dream of him for as long as it lasted.

Chapter Fifteen

*A*FTER DINNER, WHEN THE ladies retired to the drawing room, the men remained at the table to smoke cigars and partake of some excellent brandy in a sparkling crystal decanter, which was brought to the table by a servant in black and white formal attire.

The duke was the first to snip off the end of his cigar and light it. Soon they were all lounging back in their chairs in conspicuous silence.

"Am I about to be interrogated?" Drake asked, sitting forward to tap his cigar ashes into a gold-plated tray.

"Bloody well, right," Lord Vincent replied. "We heard all about your gallant rescue of our sister's reticule, but we have yet to hear the gory details. How hard did you really hit the scoundrel? Did you break anything? A nose? A jaw perhaps?"

The duke chuckled and shook his head. "Vincent, you have no shame."

"I never have, and I make no apologies. Come now, brothers, don't lie. You know you want to hear about it."

"Speak for yourself," Blake said. "I am sure Mr. Torrington doesn't wish to go into it, and certainly not at the table."

"The ladies are gone," Vincent said. "What could it hurt?"

Drake glanced at the duke who sat back leisurely in his chair with one leg crossed over the other. He and Lord Vincent shared similar looks. Each had jet-black hair and a commanding physical stature. In fact they could have been twins.

The duke shrugged a shoulder as if to suggest that Drake could speak as freely as he wished.

"I didn't break anything," Drake explained, "but the scoundrel was out cold for a good twenty minutes."

"A concussion, then," Vincent said.

"No doubt," Drake replied.

Vincent took a deep drag of his cigar, then leaned forward to tap the ashes into the tray. "Violence is a dreadful thing, but when you're a purse snatcher, you take your chances."

"Charlotte mentioned," Blake said, "that he was a gambler who owed money to the wrong people."

"That is what the constable confirmed," Drake said.

The duke also tapped his ashes in the tray. "Please allow us to thank you, Mr. Torrington, for coming to our sister's aid. She means a great deal to us."

"Naturally," Drake replied.

"So I don't need to remind you that we do not wish to see her hurt. I am not sure what you know, but she has been through some difficult times in her life."

"For pity's sake, Devon," Vincent said. "Give the man space to breathe. Charlotte is a grown woman. She can take care of herself."

There it was. The implication was clear. They all knew he and Charlotte were involved in more than just a polite acquaintance, though he suspected they would be shocked if they knew the whole truth of it. *Or perhaps not.* Lord Vincent certainly seemed a liberal sort of man. But still, Charlotte was his sister.

No one said anything for a long moment. Then Devon changed the subject. "We thought to go riding to the lake house tomorrow," he said, "and do some fishing. The ladies will join us for lunch. Do you ride, Mr. Torrington?"

"I do," Drake replied.

"Good. By the look of things, the weather promises to be fine. I predict it will be a most enjoyable day ... whether we catch salmon or not."

᏶ᏬᏉ

The following day, it rained buckets. The wind howled like a fiend over the palace rooftops. Since the fishing trip was called off, Charlotte thought carefully about how best to keep Mr. Torrington entertained, and settled upon an old family tradition—a private stroll, just the two of them, through the cold, damp, dark, and allegedly haunted palace catacombs.

"The key should be right here," she said, crouching down in the chapel to remove the loose stone in the floor in front of the choir stall. "The door to the tunnels is behind the pulpit, beyond which there is a steep set of stairs leading straight down into the very bowels of the earth. Are you up to it?"

Drake, who was holding the lantern, offered a hand to help her rise. "It sounds very romantic, Charlotte. Of course I am up to it."

She grinned at him. "Then follow me." She led him to the secret door and unlocked it with the key. He held the lamp aloft, but it lit only the first few steps. Beyond that, it was as dark as midnight at the bottom and smelled damp and musty.

"Are you mad?" he asked. "I can almost hear the rats screeching for us to come and join them."

"It's not the rats you should worry about," she said. "It's the spiders. My brothers used to torture me with them when we were children. I've had more than a few webs stuck in my hair over the years."

"Delightful," he said. "And what about the Pembroke Palace curse you mentioned when you convinced me to come here. Should I be worried?"

"Not at all. That curse was thwarted years ago." She smiled and reached for his hand. "But I did promise to tell you about it, didn't I?"

He followed her down the steep stone staircase. "You said your brothers were forced to take wives to protect their inheritances. Does that mean none of them married for love? It seems difficult to believe. They all appear to be devoted husbands today."

"They most certainly are, which is why I believe the curse was actually a blessing. Though none of us ever truly believed in that crazy old curse. We *did*, however, believe in the power of the law."

"How was that a part of it?"

They reached the bottom of the steps and began moving down the first corridor. "It's a long story," Charlotte said, "but my father ... *the duke*," she clarified, "went mad in his old age. He believed a flood was coming and that it would destroy the palace. The only way to stop it was for all of his sons to take wives before Christmas of that year. Little did we know he had changed his will to force them into it. The will was deemed valid because he was not considered mad when it was drawn up. We hired solicitors to fight it, of course, but my brothers felt it best not to risk losing that battle, so they went on a highly controlled wife hunt. I happen to believe that fate stepped in and presented the right women at exactly the right time."

"You believe in fate, then?" Drake asked.

"Yes." She believed in it absolutely. "But poor father ... he dug up the beautiful palace gardens to move his beloved roses to higher ground, and he believed the ghosts of the dead monks were haunting him at night. That was a difficult year. Once my brothers were happily married, it seemed to calm him."

Charlotte and Drake came to the end of the corridor, with branches off to either side. "This is the best way to go," she said, indicating that they should turn right. "The other way is a shorter distance, but we'd have to pass through a narrow section, and that is where I always heard the ghosts."

"I thought you said it was all just legend."

"One can never be sure," she said with a teasing smile.

They walked on. "What if the lamp goes out?" Drake said. "How will we find our way back?"

"I have matches in my pocket" she replied. "I learned a long time ago not to venture down here unprepared. In the worst case, we could escape out the other end and walk back through the rain."

And so they pressed on, holding hands, saying very little to each other after that. It was a silence that felt full and communicative, however, every so often Mr. Torrington would look at her with those arresting gray eyes and hold her in his gaze for long moments. And the occasional squeeze of her hand was a great comfort. She felt alive and euphoric, which made no sense at all, for she knew their time together was limited. Eventually she would be forced to live without him. She *should* be living in a constant state of dread.

She was no stranger to loss, however, which was perhaps why she accepted the situation. She had entered into this with a guarded heart, and come hell or high water, she would see it through with her armor intact—for what was the alternative? To put a stop to it now, just to avoid pain later on?

No, that would not do. This was far too pleasurable. She would be brave and soldier on and have wonderful memories to cling to when Drake left for America. She would treasure every precious moment of this incredible summer.

"The exit door is not far," she told him as they rounded a curve in the corridor. "There it is."

Up ahead, a small set of wooden steps led up to a heavy oaken door that was barred shut.

Drake handed the lantern to Charlotte, climbed the steps, and raised the bar. He had to shove up against it with his shoulder to push it open, for the grass had grown tall on the other side and the entrance had been cloaked in ivy for over a century.

When he pushed it open, the sun was setting and the pink light that poured in was almost blinding. He peered out, then turned around to offer his hand. Charlotte took it, climbed the steps, and bent to keep from hitting her head on the low beam over the door. Together they pushed their way through the vines and emerged into the sunset.

The forest was quiet. The rain had turned to a soft mist, and a hole in the clouds allowed glorious rays of light into the clearing. The grass and foliage sparkled with wetness. Water dripped from the trees in heavy, fat drops that beat a tattoo all around them.

Mr. Torrington closed his eyes and inhaled deeply. "I can smell the earth. How exquisite. England has its own unique fragrance, you know. Until arriving home, I didn't realize how much I missed it." His eyes searched her face.

She laid a hand on his shoulder. "Then you must enjoy it to the fullest while you are here."

Those seductive eyes were silvery blue in the mist, and she felt a stirring of arousal, for deep in her body, she sensed the heat of his desire. It was a constant between them, ever present, and she had no notion to resist it.

"How private is this place?" he asked, his voice husky and suggestive.

"Very private," she replied. "Even more so if we go that way." She pointed to a thick grove of junipers on the far side of the clearing.

He took the lantern from her, set it down by the door, then clasped her hand to lead her there.

The hem of her skirts soaked up the water as she stepped over the tangled grass, and she wondered what he had in mind, for it was too wet to lie down. When they reached a safe distance, out of sight of the ancient door, he took her into his arms and held her close until at last, his lips touched hers. It was a magical kiss that seemed to melt away the rest of the world, leaving just the two of them in this lush green garden of temptation.

He took her face in his hands, then let them roam over her body while she clutched at his broad shoulders and threw her head back in ecstasy. He kissed her throat then found her mouth again, devouring her like a starving man.

Suddenly there was a flash of light. Seconds later, a tremendous crack of thunder exploded in the heavens.

Charlotte jumped and Drake looked up at the sky as a heavy downpour began. "It's a sun shower!" she said.

"We shouldn't be out here." He grabbed her by the hand, and they laughed as they ran across the clearing. They were nearly to the door when Charlotte let go of Drake's hand and stopped.

Water dripped from his hair as he whirled around. "What are you doing?"

She was quickly becoming drenched, and her hair was falling forward into her eyes, but she had never felt such joy. She laughed again and spread her arms wide, turned in a full circle, and closed her eyes. Tipping her head back, she relished the sensation of the cool rain hitting her face.

"It's so beautiful," she said.

When she opened her eyes, he was there before her in the misty twilight. His hand settled on the curve of her hips. "We're going to get struck by lightning."

"I don't care."

Then his lips found hers again while the rain soaked through their clothing and drenched their bodies. In the end, nothing else mattered but the bliss of the moment when he backed her up against a tree, raised her skirts, efficiently worked the fastenings of his trousers, and entered her in an exhilarating rush of erotic splendor.

❧✿❧

Over the next three days, Charlotte and Drake spent every waking moment together, except for the hours when he was invited to join her brothers in some sort of manly activity that left the ladies behind. This included fishing the day after the rainstorm—the ladies merely joined them for lunch—and a game of billiards the following evening, which lasted until midnight.

As for the hours between midnight and daybreak ... they belonged solely to Charlotte and Drake, and she surrendered herself completely, without inhibition, to their passions.

When it came to lovemaking, he was a master of sensation. Those brutal hands that could kill a man in a single blow were always gentle and teasing, and he moved them over her with a grace that left her dizzy with rapture.

They spent hours exploring each other's bodies, feasting on each sensation as if every moment were the last, which was not far from the truth. But Charlotte did her best not to think of the time he would leave her. Instead, she focused on physical sensation, the flavor of his skin when she tasted him, the sound of his voice in her ear, and the glorious feel of his rippling muscles beneath her fingertips.

At times they were exhilarated in bed, relentless in their vigor. Other times, they lay exhausted on the rug before the fire, languorously sated, too tired to even speak, until he touched her a certain way, or she tasted him with her mouth. Then it would begin again—another round of sizzling hot foreplay and wildly energetic intercourse.

Caught up in the magic of those private hours alone with him, she felt as if time *could* stand still and she could remain lost in this erotic dream forever.

Nothing mattered but the ecstasy of the moment ... one after another to be savored. She refused to let the future enter her thoughts, for she wanted to remember this enchantment, perfect just as it was. Nothing would spoil it. No matter what occurred, she would have these days to remember and cherish for the rest of her life.

Chapter Sixteen

CHARLOTTE HAD LEARNED EARLY in life that all good things must eventually come to an end. When the final hour came at dawn—when it was time to leave Drake's bed and say a public good-bye to him that morning alongside her family—she gazed up at him as he lay upon her, looking into her eyes.

"I don't want you to go." She rested her hand on his cheek, rough with stubble beneath the soft flesh of her palm. "This week has been so perfect."

"Only because we didn't get caught in bed together," he said. "If I stay another day, we will most certainly be pushing our luck."

He kissed her tenderly on the mouth, and the lingering fever from her climax coursed through her blood as he withdrew from her depths.

"You will come back to London though, won't you?" he asked, as she rolled to the side. "I am here for another fortnight. I want to spend that time with you."

"I want to spend it with you as well," she replied, but secretly wished he would ask for more. What about the future beyond those two weeks? It was taking every ounce of will she possessed not to cling to him and beg him not to leave, or to ask him to take her with him—but he had made it clear from the beginning that this was a temporary affair. She did not wish him to remember her as an emotional wreck, weeping and pleading at his feet.

Instead, she took his hand in hers, kissed his palm, and pressed it to her heart. "Last night was perfect, but we both know it's time for me to return to my own rooms."

"Before we are caught," he said.

"Yes." Her body trembled with regret as she slipped out of the bed and pulled on her nightgown and robe.

"When will I see you again?" he asked.

A small part of her wanted to make him suffer, as she was suffering. What if she said she'd changed her mind and did not want to return to London after all? Would he simply say good-bye today and forget about her? Or would he decide he could not live without her, and reconsider the approaching end of this affair?

"I am not sure yet," she replied. "It may not be for a few days."

"You're killing me," he said.

Good. Because this is killing me, too.

She fastened the belt on her dressing gown and circled around the bed. "I really must go now." She was about to sweep the tapestry aside and open the secret door, when Drake rose from the bed and clasped her by the wrist.

"Wait." He pulled her into his arms and held her tight, then pressed his lips to hers.

She melted beneath the heat of the kiss. If it were not yet dawn, she would have succumbed to another hour in bed with him, but his train would be leaving in a few hours and the coachman would soon be waiting in the courtyard to deliver him to the station.

Charlotte pressed her hands to Drake's shoulders and pushed him away. "I have to go," she said, rather testily.

This time, he did not try to stop her.

༄༅༅

It was not easy to say good-bye to Pembroke. As Drake shook the duke's hand and thanked him and the duchess for their hospitality over the past few days, he understood why Charlotte had invited him here. She had wanted to show him that life could hold certain pleasures in the company of good people, and not all English aristocrats were shallow gossipmongers.

She was right. The Sinclairs were a decent bunch, fiercely loyal to one another and easy to rub along with. No wonder she was so proud of her family and happy to spend the rest of her days here. Though she had lost a great deal in her life, she would always have this. Pembroke Palace. Her home.

"It was a pleasure to have you visit us, Mr. Torrington," the duchess said. "I hope you will come again one day soon."

He said good-bye to the other siblings—Vincent and Blake, and their lovely wives—then he turned to Charlotte who stood waiting at the open door of the coach.

She looked staggeringly beautiful in the early morning sunshine. A light breeze was blowing at her skirts. The pink hue of her gown matched the color of her lips. And those eyes ... they never failed to affect him.

He kissed her hand. "Thank you again, Lady Charlotte."

"No, thank *you*, Mr. Torrington," she replied, "for the heroic rescue of my reticule."

It was all she could say, for the others were watching and listening.

Something savage in him wanted to grab her by the hand, drag her into the coach, and steal her away, but he maintained a civilized composure and simply bowed to her before stepping into the coach.

As the door was pulled shut and the vehicle began to drive away, he forced himself not to look back, for he felt agitated by the rolling of the coach wheels that took him away from her. Two weeks. That was all they had left.

Unless ...

He allowed himself to consider the possibility of something more.

ᏬᏊᏋ

Charlotte spent that day in the nursery playing with her nieces and nephews. She arranged a painting exercise with the older children that helped keep her mind occupied. Deep down, however, when she looked at the watercolor pictures, she saw Mr. Torrington's face in all of them, and was consumed by an emptiness and heavy sense of loss.

How perfect the past few days had been, talking with him and laughing, spending the nights tangled in his bed sheets, wrapped up in his strong arms while he pleasured her to the ends of the earth.

When it came time to dress for dinner that night, it all seemed like a fantasy she had concocted in vivid detail—just like in one of her novels. She knew it was real, however, for she was overcome with longing.

All the while, that old familiar misery hovered just over the horizon. She knew it all too well, and Lord knows she feared it, but she would not let it conquer her this time, as she had all those years ago. Mr. Torrington would be gone in two weeks. That was a fact. She would simply have to let go of her love and move on with her life.

If that's what it was. *Love*. She wasn't entirely sure. Perhaps it was just a very intense sexual infatuation, and when he left and the memory of it faded, so too would this feeling of loss, which at this point, too closely resembled grief.

When she entered the drawing room, her family was already gathered for drinks before dinner. Adelaide sat in a chair gazing at the floor, hardly paying attention to the conversations around her.

Charlotte approached her. Adelaide's eyes lifted and warmed instantly.

"No doubt you were sorry to see Mr. Torrington leave this morning," she said. "He is such a pleasant gentleman. We all liked him very much."

"I am pleased to hear that," Charlotte replied. "And yes, I am disappointed, but I mustn't feel sorry for myself. He is gone. That is all there is to it. In two weeks, he will be steaming his way back to America, so I had best get used to this and not set myself up to wallow in any foolish romantic imaginings."

Adelaide stared at her for a long moment. She took hold of her hand. "My darling. You know how proud I am of you for all that you have accomplished. You are one of the strongest women I know, but sometimes I worry that you are *too* formidable. You have yet to allow yourself the smallest vulnerability."

"Why should I?" Charlotte asked, surprised by her mother's sudden leap into a very intimate conversation. "I am happy with my life the way it is. I have never felt lonely or deprived."

She glanced around at the others—who thankfully weren't listening—and lowered her voice. "I don't think now is the time to be entertaining hopes for a man who has made it very clear that he is not seeking a wife. A man who intends to leave the country before the end of the month."

"But is there any chance that he might decide to stay?" Adelaide asked. "He has family here. He is an Englishman at heart."

"Yes, but he has known hard times here."

"So have you. At the same time, Charlotte ... you are free to leave if you wish."

Charlotte felt her eyebrows pull together in disbelief. "What are you up to, Mother? Are you playing matchmaker? Are you suggesting that I should pack up and steam off to America to be with him?"

"Not at all," she replied with her most charming smile. "A fresh start can be found anywhere."

Charlotte inclined her head suspiciously. "You think he should stay here?"

Adelaide shrugged, as if she did not know, either way.

Charlotte couldn't help but marvel at how things had turned out. A few short weeks ago, she had resolved to bring her parents together, as she believed they were meant to be, yet here she sat, the object of her mother's similar aspirations.

"We are too much alike, you and I," Charlotte said.

"How so?"

Charlotte gave her a look. "Don't pretend you weren't aware that I dragged you off to London to try and match you up with William. All I wanted was for you to be happy."

"And you believe that a woman requires a man in order to be happy?" Adelaide asked. "Come now, Charlotte. This is *me* you are talking to. I know you better than that."

Charlotte accepted a glass of sherry from the footman who presented it on a silver tray. She held it up, as if to toast their shared modern ideas about happiness and independence.

"I do not believe a woman requires a man to be happy," Charlotte said, "but I will not deny that the *right* man can bring about a curious and unexpected wealth of excitement in a woman's ..." She paused. "*Heart.*"

Adelaide raised her sherry glass as well. "I wholly agree."

They sipped their drinks and contemplated this universal wisdom.

"We have written to each other, you know," Adelaide said, out of the blue.

Charlotte inched a little closer on the sofa. "Who? You and William?"

"Yes. Please do not be angry, Charlotte, but I told him about your friendship with Mr. Torrington, how he helped you that day, and that we invited him to Pembroke to thank him. William was very happy for you, but our letters went somewhat beyond that. He wrote to me about his work, which I am always so very eager to hear about."

"You are back in touch with each other?" Charlotte asked. "I am so pleased to hear it."

Adelaide looked down at her lap. "I am pleased, too, but at the same time I feel uneasy."

"How so?"

"For one thing, you told me he is courting someone else, and he has been very open about it. I know it to be so, yet I still correspond with him. I cannot help but feel that is wrong. I certainly would not appreciate it if he were *my* gentleman caller and he was secretly corresponding with an old flame."

"You are not an old flame, Mother. You are much more than that. What exists between you and Dr. Thomas is a deep, lifelong love. If there is another woman involved, she is the flame that could—and should—be snuffed out."

"Charlotte," Adelaide scolded with a frown. "We know nothing about this woman or what exists between her and William. She could be deeply in love with him, while I have broken his heart time and time again. If there is any justice in the world, she shall win him, and I will have my heart stomped upon. Lord knows I deserve it."

"So you *do* feel more than friendship," Charlotte said. "But how can you say that you deserve to be miserable?"

"It is the truth. He has always been there for me, and I always took advantage, yet I never gave anything in return. I never sacrificed anything for him, and he knows it."

"Sacrifice. That is an interesting word. Do you believe it is a necessary requirement for love? Must we prove our love by giving something up? Or is it enough just to accept and give our love?"

"I have taken so much from William."

"That is not true. He must know how you respect him. Put the past behind you, Mother. If he got down on his knee today and proposed marriage, would you say yes? Would you give him your whole heart for the rest of your life?"

Adelaide's eyes lifted, and they were wet with emotion. "Yes. I would marry him tomorrow if he asked, and I would spend every waking moment making up for lost time, and thanking him for always being at my side. For putting my happiness before his own. For never betraying my trust. He is a selfless human being, and I love him for it."

Charlotte clasped her mother's hand and felt a deep stirring of certainty. Adelaide and William *were* meant to be together. Charlotte's clumsy attempt at matchmaking was not yet done for.

She thought about regret and second chances for love. About her parents.

Love was a precious thing, not to be guarded against or squandered. But isn't that what she'd advised herself to do with Drake? Wasn't she letting go of love when she should try to grasp it forever?

Suddenly her path was clear.

"Will you come back to London with me?" Charlotte asked. "I have two weeks to spend with a man I am mad about, and life is too short to throw away such precious opportunities."

"Of course I will come," her mother replied.

Later that night, Charlotte sat down at her desk to write not one, but two letters. She began with the one that would be most brief.

Dear Mr. Torrington,
I will return to London on Wednesday. May I join you at dawn the following morning for a rendezvous on the river? I will be waiting at the usual time.
-C

She sealed the letter, quickly penned the address, and set it aside.

Next she considered how best to begin the second letter, for this one was a bit more complicated, and she was rather conflicted about whether or not she should even send it. Drake had told her she shouldn't meddle in other people's love lives, but that was before he knew that the gentleman she wanted for her mother was her very own father. What would he say now? She guessed his response would be different.

Charlotte and Adelaide had been gone from London for nearly a week, and Charlotte could not bear to think that William's 'lady friend' might be sinking her hooks deeper into him with every passing moment. Charlotte needed William to know that Adelaide would be returning soon. So she began to write ...

Dear William,
I know you told me not to meddle, but there are times when a lady can do nothing but follow her heart, so meddle, I must ...

Chapter Seventeen

WILLIAM WAS TIRED AFTER his evening at the opera, for he'd been up until dawn the previous night with a patient suffering from seizures. No other physician in the city could ascertain the cause of the seizures. He had his own theories of course, but could confirm nothing at this early stage, and the family was most distraught.

His spirits were lifted, however, when he noticed two letters in the salver by the door, both of which must have been delivered while he was out.

He picked them up and recognized the penmanship on each one, and sighed with a welcome feeling of serenity. He would take both letters to the library, pour himself a brandy, and put his feet up on the upholstered stool to read them by the fire.

A short while later, he was doing just that. First, he read Adelaide's letter, for he could not resist it. He had been waiting for news about her time in Pembroke with Charlotte and her young gentleman caller. He was riveted by every word. Then he read the letter a second time.

Adelaide sounded cheerful, so much like the young girl he knew and loved in Yorkshire. It was as if not a single day stood between past and present. She was still the same, and the connection he felt to her defied reason and science.

Adelaide ... As he ran a finger over her elegant penmanship, he felt as if she were right there in this room beside him. He could feel the warmth of her presence, and he almost believed she could read his thoughts from afar. That somehow she knew he was reading her letter at this very moment, and she was thinking of him, as he was thinking of her.

Then William thought of Dorothea and pinched the bridge of his nose. He took a deep swig of the brandy, set down the glass, and opened Charlotte's letter.

> Dear Dr. Thomas,
> I know you told me not to meddle, but there
> are times when a lady can do nothing but
> follow her heart, so meddle, I must. Mother
> and I have decided to return to London on
> Wednesday.

William's heart leapt. *That was tomorrow. He continued to read.*

> I am not certain how long we will stay,
> but I suspect a fortnight or so. There is
> another reason for my letter, however. I felt I
> must reveal an important truth to you.
> I still remember what you said to me
> in your office the last time I visited, and
> I understand that you have moved on
> with your life and do not wish to return
> to an existence of hopeless dreams and
> disappointments. I understand it very well,
> for you and I have both been forced to build
> fortresses around our hearts. We do not

dare to dream or fight for a happy ending, for we know too well the unbearable agony of such a defeat.

So I write to tell you this vital fact, my dear, beloved father ... There will be no defeat this time, only triumph if you choose to seize it. I spoke to Mother this evening, and she told me that she would marry you tomorrow if you asked. She loves you, William, and always has.

Yes, I am betraying her confidence by revealing this to you, for she does not know I am writing, but I am certain that she will forgive me if it brings the two of you together at last. I simply could not risk the possibility that you might take steps in another direction if you did not know the full truth and have a chance to contemplate the absolute certainty of your success.

She loves you, as do I. Now it is up to you to choose your path. Whatever you decide, I will honor it. I will embrace your lady if she is the one you truly want, but I could not let you move forward without knowing all the relevant particulars.

—Charlotte

William set down the letter, gazed into the dancing flames of the fire, and wept uncontrollably.

When he recovered his composure, he poured himself another drink and pondered the two letters he had just received.

There was still a part of him that was angry with Adelaide for all the pain she had caused him throughout his life, and for betraying the undying love that had existed between them—at least on his side. A part of him wanted to disappoint her, but that was his pride bucking.

All his life he had been there for Adelaide, steady and devoted, forgiving her for the choices she had made. But had it really been her choice to marry the duke? She had once told him she'd had none, and he did believe that she walked down the aisle only to save him from her father's brutality. If only she could have trusted William to survive and come to her rescue.

But he had not come to her rescue, had he? Not after she signed her name to that marriage certificate. Instead he had fled the country and thrown himself into a pit of rage and despair. Oh, how he had loathed her at times. So much so that he had left her to the duke, who had turned her life into a living hell. Perhaps William should have returned for her instead of leaving ...

So who was to blame for their separation? For all the lost years? They'd both played their parts, contributed to the sorrow, yet here they were, decades later, and life was not so wretched. Adelaide had raised five beautiful children, and he had been free to devote his entire life to the study of science and medicine. He was pleased with what he had accomplished, and he knew Adelaide would never regret the life she had lived.

What path should he choose?

He thought of Dorothea again, who had been such an agreeable companion this Season. She was in love with him. There was no question about it, and he had been flattered by her attentions. But he did not love her in return. Not as he loved Adelaide, the true mate of his soul.

Yes. There it was. The truth in all its radiant glory. Adelaide was his one true love.

Better to end it now with Dorothea, before promises were made.

Oh, Lord. He knew exactly how it felt to be rejected.

He would not enjoy hurting her.

かごか

Dorothea Torrington had just handed her opera cloak over to the butler when she spotted a letter on the table in the hall. She moved quickly to pick it up, read the return address, then slipped it into the folds of her gown and said, "Is my son at home?"

"No, madam. He has been out all evening."

"I see. And when did the mail arrive?"

"A private courier came an hour ago."

"Very good. Thank you. Will you have Mrs. March send up some claret and warm biscuits?"

"Right away."

A few minutes later, she was alone in her boudoir, unfolding the letter addressed to her son.

Dear Mr. Torrington,
I will return to London on Wednesday and would like to join you at dawn the following morning for another rendezvous on the river. I will be waiting at the usual time.
—C

Wednesday? That was tomorrow! Dorothea clenched her jaw and crumpled the letter furiously in a fist. A rendezvous at dawn ... It was just as she suspected—a torrid affair that could quite possibly ruin everything.

Oh, how could Drake be such a fool? He was here for the summer only. What was he thinking, becoming involved in *that* way with the daughter of a duke?

More importantly, the daughter of Adelaide Sinclair, Dowager Duchess of Pembroke, of all people.

Oh yes, Dorothea knew the history behind the dowager's acquaintance with William. Recently Dorothea had watched him dance with Adelaide at the Halloway Ball, had seen the spark of familiarity between them, and the attraction. There had been some whisperings of a former courtship between them. According to London gossip, they had been raised on neighboring estates in Yorkshire and were once promised to each other ... All speculation of course.

No, no, no! Dorothea massaged her temples. Drake could not continue with this affair!

Dorothea paced back and forth in front of the fire while her blood blazed hotter than the flames in the hearth. This sordid connection to the daughter of William's old flame simply could not continue. Drake must leave England immediately and return to America. There was no reason for him to stay. Their finances were secured, and she certainly did not need him for anything else. He had to leave London, and Lady Charlotte needed to take her mother straight back to the country dower house where she bloody well belonged.

Drake would *not* be meeting Lady Charlotte for a wicked rendezvous on the river tomorrow. Not if Dorothea had anything to do with it.

Overcome by a jealous rage, she threw the letter into the fire and watched it burn to ash.

Chapter Eighteen

CHARLOTTE WAS AWAKE WITH the birds on Thursday morning. She dressed without ringing for her maid and tiptoed downstairs to watch for Mr. Torrington's coach through the front window.

Her heart beat fast when a vehicle pulled into the square, but it was not Mr. Torrington, and she sighed with disappointment and impatience.

It seemed like forever since they had parted at the palace, and she longed for him desperately. It was the worst sort of deprivation. She was miserable one minute and bursting with excitement the next. Before her carriage left Pembroke Palace for the station, it had been all she could do to keep from saddling a horse and galloping all the way to London on her own to see him again.

At last, the waiting was over. He would be here soon and she would run out to his coach and throw herself into his arms. She had been dreaming of such a moment for days. Perhaps she would tell him how she truly felt—that this had become more than just a casual affair to her. Somewhere along the way, she had fallen quite madly in love with him.

Could she dare say it? *Should* she? Or would it frighten him away?

No, she decided, it would make him smile. She was certain of it, for she remembered the tenderness of his lovemaking at Pembroke, especially that evening in the rain at sunset.

He had teased her once about a forced marriage between them. It had been a hint. He wouldn't have said such a thing if he hadn't at least thought about a future with her. Men didn't joke about matters of marriage unless they were serious and inclined.

Growing impatient, Charlotte glanced up at the clock on the wall. It was nearly quarter past six. It wasn't like him to be late. He had never been late for any of their secret meetings before.

She forced herself to take a seat and wait patiently. Every sound outside in the square brought her to her feet to peer out the window, but it was always the same—a milk cart or a merchant delivering fish, meat, or dry goods.

The next half hour was pure hell.

When the clock chimed seven o'clock, Charlotte rose from her chair one last time with a heavy, aching heart.

Mr. Torrington was not coming.

He did not wish to see her.

There was nothing to do but go back upstairs and ring for an early breakfast.

But why had he not come? And why didn't he send a note, saying so? Wondering about his absence, Charlotte climbed the stairs. Had she been mistaken about the sincerity of his affections? Or was it possible that he had not received her letter?

 తురితో

By twelve noon, Charlotte couldn't bear another moment of not knowing. Her mother had gone off to a hospital charity event, and Charlotte had been left behind to wonder what had happened to Mr. Torrington that morning. Had he indeed not received her letter, or was this his way of sending her a message to communicate that the summer was almost over, and it was time to bring a swift, clean end to their affair?

For all she knew he may have already departed for America. Perhaps she had pushed too hard at Pembroke, behaved too much like a woman in love, and he had recognized the depth of her emotions. She was not the sort of woman who loved halfheartedly. When she gave her heart, she gave it with all her might. Perhaps they should call her The Iron Fist as well, for she was no lightweight lover. She fairly hit the roof when she was at the height of her passions.

But just as she was passionate, she was also honest and forthcoming. If Mr. Torrington wanted to end it, she needed to know, for she was a master at moving on with her life. And she deserved to be told, face to face. She had been preparing herself all along—*steeling* herself—for the end of their affair since the moment it began. So she simply needed to know. Was this the end? Or had his coach broken an axle on the way to her house?

At two o'clock, she had the driver bring the curricle around to take her to Mr. Torrington's London townhouse, for Charlotte could not go another moment without knowing the answers to those questions.

❦

The last time Charlotte entered this house, she had come through the front door in a strange man's arms, like a bride on her wedding night, with one notable difference—she had been bleeding from the head.

Today she had all her wits about her, but felt as if her heart were bleeding as she was shown into the parlor to meet Mr. Torrington's mother, who rose with the utmost politeness. She invited Charlotte to take a seat, then offered her a cup of tea.

"How is your head, Lady Charlotte?" Mrs. Torrington asked as she poured the steaming tea into the cup. "What a horrendous ordeal it must have been for you. I am relieved the culprit is in custody."

Charlotte was not at all sorry to be meeting Drake's mother this afternoon, for she had wondered what sort of woman she was. Drake had spoken of the rift that existed between them, which Charlotte found most troubling. She couldn't imagine not seeing her own mother for twelve years.

Perhaps there was a way to bridge that gap somehow. Though she supposed she was looking to meddle again, wasn't she ...?

Charlotte smiled at Mrs. Torrington and couldn't help but sense something familiar about her. She was certainly an attractive woman with thick, wavy dark hair, very much like Drake's. Her eyes were a slivery blue as well, and she possessed an uncommon beauty that made it difficult not to stare.

Perhaps her familiarity was simply a result of the fact that she was Drake's mother, and Charlotte could see him in her eyes.

"Indeed," Charlotte replied as she accepted the cup and saucer and took the first sip. "I cannot thank you enough for your son's assistance and for your housekeeper's kindness that day. I don't know what I would have done otherwise."

"It is all in the past now," Mrs. Torrington said as she regarded Charlotte with a narrowing gaze over the gold rim of her teacup.

An awkward silence ensued. Charlotte quickly filled it with some polite conversation. "You have a lovely home," she said. "I quite like the colors you have chosen for the walls in this room. It is very cozy."

"Thank you for the compliment," Mrs. Torrington coolly replied and sat back in her chair.

Charlotte felt as if an iceberg had just floated into the parlor, though perhaps it had been there all along. Was the woman naturally aloof? Or did she have some reason to dislike Charlotte?

Perhaps it was the fact that Charlotte was making love to her son. Good God. Did she know?

Charlotte swallowed uneasily and set her teacup down on the table. "Is Mr. Torrington at home?" she asked. "I came to wish him well before he leaves for America."

Mrs. Torrington tapped one long fingernail on the arm of her chair and regarded Charlotte with unmistakable derision. "No, my son is not at home, and you should count yourself lucky that he is not."

"Why is that?" Charlotte asked.

The woman glared at her. "Because he is not the sort of man with whom a lady like *you* should keep company."

The walls seemed to suddenly close in around Charlotte. "I don't understand."

Mrs. Torrington sat forward again and scoffed. "Surely you know that he has a violent streak. You must have seen it for yourself when you were robbed and he stopped the thief from getting away. It's why he left here all those years ago, because the entire country knew what he was capable of. He would most certainly have ended up in prison, or dead, if he had stayed."

"That was a long time ago," Charlotte argued in his defense. "From what I understand, it was a difficult time for him."

He had just lost his wife. He had taken his grief out in the boxing ring, while Charlotte had dealt with her own grief by hiding away from the world and despising it. People changed with the passing of time and new life experiences. She was not the same woman now. He, too, had changed. She had recovered and she was stronger. She believed Drake had also found peace again. "And I do not believe he has a violent streak. I believe he is a good man."

Mrs. Torrington stood up. "Lady Charlotte, you are not hearing me."

Charlotte also stood. "What is it, exactly, that you wish me to hear, madam? I prefer frank words, if you please."

They stared at each other fixedly.

"Very well, then," Mrs. Torrington said. "I know all about your secret meetings with my son. Obviously I am shocked and scandalized by the nature of your acquaintance. I assure you he did not come home to enter into a cheap and torrid affair with a desperate spinster. He has been through enough. Therefore I respectfully suggest that you end it immediately and keep away from him, otherwise you will soon find your reputation in ruins—whatever is left of it—when word of this gets out. I advise you to return to the country and stay there. For pity's sake, Lady Charlotte, go home and behave yourself."

Charlotte frowned with disbelief. "How dare you."

Mrs. Torrington's cheeks turned red. "It's over. He doesn't want to see you anymore."

"I don't believe you. Where is he?"

"Oh, dear girl. Spare yourself the humiliation. Go back to Pembroke and forget him."

Feeling numb with shock, Charlotte stared vigilantly at Mrs. Torrington. This made no sense at all. Charlotte was not some cheap harlot. She was the daughter of a duke! Perhaps Mrs. Torrington was simply a controlling woman who could not bear for her son to be happy on his own. Or perhaps she truly was scandalized by Charlotte's modern attitudes and self-reliance—both sexually and socially—for Charlotte was independent, and had earned her own fortune through her creative ingenuity.

"I believe we are done here," Charlotte said. "Good day, Mrs. Torrington." She turned and walked out.

It was not until she climbed into the curricle that she paused to consider all the hideous things that woman had just said to her.

'He doesn't want to see you ... Spare yourself the humiliation.'

Charlotte remembered how she had felt that morning when Drake did not arrive to take her rowing on the river. Was it true? Was she a desperate spinster, blind to the fact that he had only wanted her for one thing, and now he was done with her?

She squeezed her reticule in her hands. *No.* She would not accept that.

Yes, her heart had become involved, which had never been part of the plan. But so had his. She was certain of it. His mother was wrong.

Oh, God! Charlotte had wanted so badly to admire the woman—and for the feeling to be mutual—for she was Drake's mother. The person who had brought him into the world. The reason he'd returned to England.

She was his *mother*.

Why was she so dreadfully mean?

Charlotte slumped back in her seat, barely able to comprehend what just happened. And what in the world was she going to do about it?

Chapter Nineteen

*A*DELAIDE WASN'T SURE IF she would see William that afternoon at the Ladies' Hospital Auxiliary Garden Party. She had mentioned in her last letter that she would be attending, but she had not heard back from him. Nevertheless, she had donned her most flattering afternoon dress—a slim-fitting coral affair with a light draping about the skirt, and a collar of antique lace with a fashionable hat and matching fan.

To her surprise, William was giving a speech about the new hospital wing just as she arrived. The sound of his voice—so deep and authoritative—made her feel as if she stood on shaky ground.

In all these years, he had not lost his masculine appeal, and his intelligence was still overwhelmingly attractive to her. For years she had buried her awareness of him as a man, for she was a married woman and that had decided her path. But something had changed this summer. They were older now, but oh, she felt like a young girl again in his presence. Her belly turned somersaults and her heart fluttered like a butterfly.

His gaze found hers just as he finished the speech. There was a round of muted gloved applause on the sunny lawn. Then he disappeared into the crowd to speak to the hosts and other officials.

A short while later, a footman came by and offered Adelaide a glass of lemonade. She took it from the shiny tray and clicked open her fan to cool her cheeks.

"Your Grace ..." William's voice brushed over her like a refreshing breeze off the water. She turned and faced him.

"How wonderful to see you, William. Your speech was very inspiring."

"I'm glad you came," he said.

His eyes sparkled in the sunlight and she was overcome by a deep affection for him, which rose up within her like an overflowing cup of wine. If there had been any doubt in her mind that she loved this man as much, if not more, than she loved him in her youth, it was gone now. Her true feelings were no longer smothered beneath her sense of duty and all the painful regrets of the past. All of that was behind her now as she stood before him on this bright, shimmering summer's day.

"Would you care to take a walk over to the dessert table?" he asked. "They tell me there is a cake large enough to feed all of Mayfair."

Adelaide smiled and slipped her arm through his. "That sounds positively delicious."

As they walked together, they spoke of things they had corresponded about in their daily letters. Adelaide asked about his patients, and he asked about Charlotte's gentleman caller.

"He was delightful," Adelaide said. "We all thought the world of him, and he beat Vincent at billiards, which impressed everyone significantly. But the most wonderful part was the joy I saw in Charlotte's eyes every time they were together. I have not seen her look so happy in years. She came alive again, William. I only hope something will come of it, and she won't be disappointed."

"Love can be unpredictable," he said, "but Charlotte is an extraordinary woman and very strong. Whatever happens, I have every confidence that she will find what she is looking for. She has so much bounty in her life. I am proud of her. You raised her well, Adelaide."

They reached the dessert table and Adelaide let go of his arm. Another footman served them each a slice of lemon cake on small china plates. They wandered off to enjoy it beneath the shade of a tall sycamore tree.

While they talked of different things, Adelaide began to feel all tangled up inside. He had always been a devoted friend to her. And now it looked like that's all he would ever wish to be.

Before she realized what she was saying—she really should have thought it through—she was clearing her throat and setting down her fork. "Do you have plans for dinner this evening?" she asked. "It is only Charlotte, Garrett, and me at the London house. We would love for you to join us."

For a number of seconds that moved slower than chilled honey, he gave no reply. Adelaide wanted to disappear under the dessert table.

"I appreciate the invitation," William said at last, "but I do have plans. I have theater tickets with ... a friend."

Adelaide knew instantly that he was seeing his lady tonight. She could see it in his eyes, hear it in his voice—for she knew him too well. He felt awkward and uncomfortable. She simply couldn't bear it.

"Perhaps another time, then," she courteously replied. "Charlotte and Garrett always love to see you."

Nothing was quite the same after that, and Adelaide wanted to kick herself for imagining that they could ever go back to what they once were. She was a grown woman, not some young debutante—and how many times had she told herself there was too much history that could not be undone?

Lord knows she deserved this disappointment. She deserved to be jilted by William for all the times she had given him hope, only to disappoint, to go back to the duke.

It was time to let this go, she decided. To let William go. She had chosen her path many years ago. Now she must live with that choice.

ᘒᘯᘒ

"Mother, you look like you've been trampled by a herd of cattle," Charlotte said when she entered the drawing room before dinner. "What happened? Your eyes are all puffy."

"It's nothing," Adelaide replied, dabbing at them with a handkerchief.

"Don't say it's nothing when clearly something is wrong. Please tell me." Charlotte took hold of Adelaide's hand.

At last, her mother explained. "Very well, then. If you must know, I am not as indifferent about William seeing this other woman as I have led you to believe. I saw him at the garden party today, and my heart nearly beat out of my chest. He was so handsome. So charming."

Charlotte squeezed her mother's hand and gently laughed. "That comes as no shock to me, Mother. I never believed you were indifferent. Not for a single second."

"Well," she replied, "I am going to have to learn to be, for I made a fool of myself today."

"How so?"

"I invited him to join us for dinner, and there was an excruciating silence while he looked at me with regret. Then he told me he couldn't come because he had other plans with his ... *lady friend.*" She sucked in a shaky breath. "Oh, look at me. What a fool I am. You would think, at my age ..."

"Don't be silly, Mother. You are as youthful as you ever were, and are you certain he was seeing his lady friend tonight? Perhaps it was something else. Something to do with a patient at the hospital."

Adelaide shook her head. "No, he mentioned theater tickets. I could sense what it was, and he knew I did."

Charlotte sat back and sighed. How disappointing. She had hoped her letter to William might change things, but perhaps she was a bigger fool than anyone with all her lofty dreams of happy endings, for both herself and her parents. Like Adelaide, Charlotte's day had been most unpleasant—and still, there was no word from Drake. She felt rejected and humiliated. And angry—mostly with his beastly mother.

Was Drake aware of his mother's knowledge of their affair? Had he known the sorts of things she intended to say to Charlotte? She struggled to give him the benefit of the doubt, even while the sensible part of her brain was telling her to give up hope.

Perhaps she and Adelaide *should* go back to Pembroke Palace and ponder lessons learned.

"It appears both of our matchmaking schemes have turned out to be colossal failures," Charlotte said.

"What do you mean?"

"I went to see Mr. Torrington today, but he was not at home. At least I do not think he was. Instead I met his mother, who told me that he didn't want to see me anymore, and I should go back to Pembroke and forget about him. She also warned me that he had a violent streak. Then she called me a desperate spinster."

"She did not!"

"She *did*."

Adelaide took a moment to consider this information. In the end, her reaction was peaceful, as it always was. "Oh my dear," she said. "I know it is difficult, but you must find a way to be compassionate and forgiving. Mrs. Torrington must be an unhappy woman indeed to say such things to you. We do not know what kind of life she has led, for we have not walked in her shoes. Perhaps she is lonely and is afraid of losing her son."

Charlotte shook her head doubtfully. "Her son, who has been out of the country for twelve years? No, I do not think that is it. And I was certainly *not* compassionate this afternoon. I was furious with her. By some miracle I managed to keep a cool head, and I walked out."

Her mother sighed. "I am proud of you for keeping your head. That is what matters."

Charlotte leaned close and kissed her mother on the cheek. "If you only knew how much I admire you ... You are the best woman I know."

"If only William thought so," Adelaide said with a sigh that broke Charlotte's heart.

She squeezed her hand again. "If he doesn't think so, then he is not as brilliant as we think he is. He is a complete imposter, I'd say."

Adelaide managed a smile.

Charlotte remembered telling William that she would honor his choice, whatever it was, but that would be easier said than done if he chose the other woman.

Charlotte wondered what the other woman looked like. Was she as charming, beautiful, and kind-hearted as Adelaide?

The woman must be truly fabulous indeed, if William were inclined to take her as his first choice.

ᘏᘏᘏ

It was almost nine o'clock when Drake arrived home and stepped out of his coach. Looking up at the townhouse with all the windows ablaze with light, he tried to recall a time in the past when he was happy here, but could not. His childhood had been colored by abuse, for he had a bully for a father and a mother who had been too frightened to stand up to him, even for her son.

Then his adulthood was darkened by grief following the deaths of his sisters and the loss of his beloved wife—the woman who had pulled him out of all the wretchedness and shown him love and happiness for the first time. The pain of that loss had been impossible to bear.

Thus followed years of violence in the boxing ring, the barbaric cheering of the crowd when bones cracked and blood splattered ...

Purging those memories from his mind, he took in a deep breath of clean summer air, and reminded himself that that life was behind him now. He had traveled to America to cleanse himself of it and wipe the slate clean. The past twelve years had done just that, and here he was, home again—and miraculously, it felt like he was being offered a new beginning.

He reached into his pocket and pulled out the small velvet bag. Slipping his fingers into the drawstring opening, he withdrew the diamond ring he had purchased that afternoon and tried to imagine what he would say to Charlotte when he presented it to her.

More importantly, what would *she* say?

He looked up at the front of the house again. Perhaps everything was about to change. Perhaps this could be a place of joy after all.

When he climbed the steps and opened the door, however, the terrible sound of woeful sobs hit him like a bag of rocks and sent his stomach into a whirlwind of dread. He had heard his mother weep like that only once before—when his sisters slipped away, both of them, in a single afternoon.

Drake was startled by the appearance of the butler before him.

"Welcome home, Mr. Torrington," the man said, as if nothing were amiss. "May I take your hat?"

Drake quickly removed it and handed it over. "What has happened?"

"I do not believe it is my place to say, sir. Your mother is in her boudoir if you wish to see her."

Drake thanked him and climbed the stairs, taking two at a time to the top. He rapped a knuckle on the door. "Mother, may I come in?"

The wailing stopped instantly and he waited, tensely, for her to respond.

The door opened and she stood before him with tear-stained cheeks, a red nose, and tousled hair.

"Good God. Are you all right?" Drake asked.

"No!" she sobbed and returned to the bed. She climbed onto it, curled up on her side, and blew her nose.

"You must tell me what happened." Drake followed her inside and circled around the bed. He pulled up a chair. "What can I do?"

"Nothing!" she cried. "No one can do anything. It is a lost cause."

"What is?"

"My happiness. Dr. Thomas came to escort me to the theater tonight, but then he walked into the parlor and told me that it would be best if we did not go after all, for he did not wish to toy with my affections any longer."

"I beg your pardon?"

Dorothea sat up and threw her handkerchief over the foot of the bed. "He ended our courtship! I will never see him again!"

"Why?" Drake asked. He was under the impression they would soon be engaged. It was one of the reasons he had come home—to secure his mother's finances and to meet Doctor Thomas and assure himself that the man was not a fortune hunter. That he was a decent and honorable fellow. Drake had met him on three separate occasions and had satisfied himself that the doctor was all of those things. He then made sure his mother would continue to maintain control of her own money, which Drake had placed in trust for her.

He had thought very highly of Dr. Thomas and had no reason to suspect he would behave in such an ungentlemanly manner.

Drake stood up and squeezed his hands into fists. "This happened tonight?"

"Yes. An hour ago."

"Did he give you any explanation? Did he not realize there was an understanding between you?"

"No! Yes! I don't know! I was so shocked, I cannot even remember what he said!"

Drake's blood began to boil. How could he have misjudged Dr. Thomas and taken him for a man of honor? To lead his mother down a merry path all Season long, and to encourage her affections … It went beyond the pale.

Drake strode toward the door.

"Where are you going?" his mother cried.

"Out."

ᘏꙩᘒ

Bang! Bang! Bang!

Drake pounded on the door to Dr. Thomas's medical offices, knowing full well that the man was not there, for all the windows were dark. He continued to pound because it took the edge off.

Next Drake tried the doctor's private residence in Mayfair, but was told he was at the theater with Mrs. Torrington. The servants had no idea when he might return and were baffled to learn that Dr. Thomas was not, in fact, at the theater with Drake's mother. Which was exactly why Drake was so insistent upon seeing him.

With growing frustration, Drake returned to his coach, climbed inside, and tapped his fingers upon his thigh. He had come home from the jeweler with high hopes for a pleasant trip to Pembroke Palace in the morning, but this disagreeable business had cast a large, dark shadow over his mood. His mother was in tears and heartbroken. How could he board a train in the morning and leave her behind, while he went to propose to a woman she did not approve of?

But did his mother's lack of approval even matter? Did he owe her anything? She had done nothing all those years ago when his father drank too much and beat Drake to a pulp.

But bloody hell, she was his mother, and she had suffered too.

Perhaps Drake could hold off going to Pembroke Palace for a day or two, at least until she stopped weeping. Then she might be able to accept his news and be happy for him.

The coach lurched forward, but since they were in Mayfair already, he lowered the glass and shouted out the window, "Drive past Pembroke House, if you please."

"Yes, sir," his coachman replied.

It was a silly thing to do, for Charlotte was still in the country, but Drake needed to feel some connection to her. He wanted to remember those promising moments of anticipation when she walked out the front door to join him for an early morning row on the Thames.

This turmoil with his mother and her broken dreams had knocked him off kilter. What if his own dreams were at risk as well? What if Charlotte did not share his feelings and refused his proposal? What would he do then?

Good God. None of this emotional drama was the least bit familiar to him. He had been living a reclusive life and had expected to remain a bachelor until he drew his last breath. What had changed? What had happened to him? He was The Iron Fist, after all.

Why was he feeling so bloody sentimental? And so damned vulnerable?

The coach pulled into the square where he had come to collect Charlotte at dawn on those two previous occasions. Just the memory of those mornings made his heart skip a beat. Clearly, he had tumbled over the edge, well beyond sexual attraction and infatuation, into a full-blown love affair that made him feel as if he walked on a cloud.

Then, when he saw the house all lit up, his hopes soared and his heart began to beat wildly. Was she here? Had she returned to London without telling him? Had she not been able to stay away?

He stood up in the coach and rapped a fist on the ceiling. "Stop here!"

The coach pulled to a halt and Drake opened the door.

Chapter Twenty

One hour earlier ...

*A*DELAIDE, CHARLOTTE, AND GARRETT had retired to the drawing room after dinner and were just about to begin a game of cards when the butler walked in.

"There is a gentleman here to see you, Your Grace. I took the liberty of showing him into the library."

"Who is it?" Adelaide asked.

"Dr. William Thomas."

A swarm of butterflies invaded Adelaide's belly, and her gaze met Charlotte's. "What is he doing here at this hour?"

"Wasn't he supposed to be at the theater tonight?" Charlotte asked.

Garrett sat back in his chair. "What is going on? You are both behaving as if William is here to catch you robbing a bank."

Adelaide struggled to regain her composure and smiled at her son. "Forgive me, Garrett. I didn't expect him. That is all. I will go downstairs and see what he wants."

Garrett began to shuffle and deal the cards onto the table. "Invite him up. We could use a fourth player."

She cleared her throat nervously and lifted her eyebrows at Charlotte, who was equally flustered.

"I will be back shortly," she said.

Adelaide descended the stairs slowly, for her heart was all aflutter and she was a bouncing ball of nerves. Why was William here, and for pity's sake ... how did she look? Was her hair all right? Perhaps she should go to her room first and check her appearance in the cheval glass, and take a moment to collect herself.

Then all at once Adelaide found herself standing outside the library door. She felt a strange mixture of euphoria and emotional agony, for the thought of him loving another woman was worse than death.

She paused outside the door, swallowed hard, then entered cheerfully with a warm smile. "William, what a lovely surprise."

He was facing the fire, but turned quickly when she spoke. Still dressed in formal black and white theater attire, he looked as frazzled as she felt. She had never seen such an anxious expression on his face before. There was something happy in his eyes, however ... though he looked shaken, as if he'd nearly been run over by a turnip cart.

"Please accept my apologies for the intrusion," he said. "I hope I am not interrupting anything."

"Not at all," she replied, crossing the room to stand before him. "You are always welcome. You know that. Especially when Charlotte and Garrett are here." *Our beautiful children.* "They asked me to invite you upstairs for cards. Will you join us?"

A calmness spread over her suddenly as William removed his spectacles, folded them, and slipped them into the breast pocket of his jacket.

"You know I love a good card game as much as the next man," he said, "but I came here to see *you,*

Adelaide. In private. There is something I wish to ask you."

She tried to breathe steadily. She did not know what to expect.

Then suddenly he dropped down on one knee and clasped both her hands in his. Bright, shimmering hope, precious and thrilling, exploded within her like a burst of starlight.

"Adelaide," he said, his voice soft and low as he looked up at her. "I have known you all my life, and I have loved you all that time. There has never been any woman for me but you, and that is why I could never leave your side, even when you belonged to another. I have waited a long time, and I would have waited forever if I had to, but the time for waiting is over." And he paused.

"You are the other half of my soul," he continued at last, "and I want you now, for myself, utterly and completely. I want to hold you in my arms, worship you every day for the rest of my life, and give you all the happiness and pleasure I am capable of giving. I want to grow old with you, Adelaide, and never be without you."

He pulled her hands to his lips and kissed her knuckles, and her whole being filled with a joy she had not imagined could exist.

"Will you marry me, Adelaide," he asked, "and end my lifelong yearning? Will you make me the happiest man alive?"

"Oh, William," she sighed, as he reached into his pocket and withdrew a stunning square-cut ruby ring surrounded by diamonds.

"May I put this on you?" he asked.

Her hand trembled as she held it out. "Yes. Yes!"

His eyes glimmered with something that resembled flirtatious amusement, and he slid the ring onto her finger. It fit perfectly.

"I am so happy," she cried laughingly as he rose to his full height before her. She stood up on her toes and wrapped her arms around his neck. "I love you so very much, my darling! I thought I would die if you married another, because I always believed you were mine. All I want is to be yours at last, for I am tired of waiting, too." She drew back to hold his face in her hands. "We were dutiful and good, and patient, were we not?"

"Yes," he replied. "I have admired and respected your integrity, Adelaide. You were a magnificent duchess and the best mother in the world."

"But now I am free to be with you," she said. "There is a new, very capable duchess at Pembroke now—lovely Rebecca, who has taken hold of the reins admirably—and all my children are grown. It is time I took something for myself, and that something is *you*, the man I have always adored. Dreamed of. Do you mean it, William? Are we finally going to be together?"

"I will never let anyone or anything tear us apart again," he replied.

He pulled her close and held her for a perfect shuddering moment of elation before he pressed his lips to hers.

All at once, Adelaide was swept back in time to that profound moment years ago, on the eve of her wedding, when he kissed her in the maze beneath the light of the moon and convinced her that they were destined to be together. She had believed it and was willing to give up everything for him that night, but that was not to be. Not then.

Everything was different now, however. Here he was, kissing her again, as if not a single moment, or hour, or year had been lost.

He drew back and smiled at her in the golden glow of the firelight. "You are to be mine, at last," he whispered.

She blinked up at him in awe, nodded, and remembered her tears from earlier that day.

"But what about your lady friend?" she asked. "I thought you had plans with her this evening."

"I spoke to her and explained I could not escort her to the theater tonight, or any other night for that matter—for my affections were engaged elsewhere."

"Oh dear," Adelaide replied. "She must have been devastated. I am so sorry."

"I was sorry, too," he said, "but she will recover. It was only a summer courtship, and we really didn't know each other very well. It was not like it is between you and me."

"Sometimes I feel as if you are living inside my own heart," Adelaide said.

"I feel it, too," he replied.

A knock sounded at the front door. Adelaide turned to see the butler pass by the library to answer it.

"Who could that be?" she said.

They listened as the caller was greeted, then the butler passed by the library door again to head upstairs.

"Someone must be here to see Charlotte or Garrett," Adelaide said, wondering—hoping—that it might be Mr. Torrington, here to apologize for his mother's unseemly conduct.

Sure enough, Charlotte passed by the library door next, and there was some hushed conversation in the entrance hall before she appeared on the threshold. "Look, Mother," she said. "We have a guest. Mr. Torrington is here."

He stepped into view as well, and Adelaide immediately went to greet him. "How lovely to see you, Mr. Torrington. Please come in. Allow me to introduce my ..." She paused. "This is my fiancé, Dr. William Thomas. William, this is Mr. Drake Torrington, the gentleman who came to Charlotte's rescue when she was attacked by the thief a few weeks ago."

Charlotte laughed out loud. "Fiancé?"

Adelaide smiled and nodded. "Yes."

"Oh, Mother, that is wonderful news!" Charlotte hugged her.

Meanwhile, Mr. Torrington was slowly moving into the library, frowning at William, who regarded him with astonishment. Neither made a move to shake hands.

Charlotte and Adelaide exchanged uneasy glances.

"Do you two know each other?" Charlotte asked.

Mr. Torrington raked a hand through his hair. "Yes, I am afraid we do."

Chapter Twenty-one

CHARLOTTE LAID A HAND on Drake's sleeve. "Is something wrong?"

He shook his head in disbelief. Then he frowned at her. "Is this the successful result of your matchmaking?"

She stammered slightly. "I ... I am not sure. It appears so." She turned to William. "You two are really getting married?"

"Yes," he said.

Charlotte hurried to hug him. "I am so happy for you both. Congratulations."

"Wait a minute," Drake said. "Before you all run off to celebrate, I will have you know that I just spent the past hour consoling my mother, who was, a short time ago, jilted by this man without any explanation whatsoever. So this is what you have been up to, is it?" he said to William. "Carrying on liaisons with two women at once? Do you have any idea the hurt you have caused?"

Charlotte looked down at Drake's fists clenching and flexing, and felt a sickening dread roll over her.

"I don't understand what you are implying," Charlotte said. "Do you mean to suggest that the woman Dr. Thomas has been courting was *your mother?*"

His angry gaze shot to hers. "Yes."

Charlotte backed away from Drake, then looked up at William, the man who was her real father *and* her mother's lifelong love. As she recalled Mrs. Torrington's cruelty earlier that day, she simply could not think of herself. "Well," she said decisively, "if he has extricated himself from that relationship, I can only say *bravo.*"

"I beg your pardon?" Drake replied.

She squared her shoulders. "Allow me to explain. Today I had the pleasure of meeting your mother. Did she not tell you? I paid a call, you see, hoping to learn why you ignored my letter and did not wish for me to join you on the river this morning. But that is beside the point. What matters is that your mother was grossly disrespectful to me."

"How so?" he asked.

"She informed me that you had not come home to take part in a ... what was the word she used? Oh yes, a 'torrid' affair. She called me a desperate spinster and told me to go back to the country and spare myself any further humiliation where you are concerned."

Drake's lips pressed together in an angry grimace.

William's head drew back in surprise. "She said that to you? Are we speaking of the same woman? Dorothea Torrington?"

"Yes," Charlotte replied. "She treated me like dirt on the underside of her boot. And *you* ..." She turned to Drake again. "You left me humiliated indeed! I waited until seven o'clock this morning, but clearly you preferred to row alone."

No one said anything for a full ten seconds. The fire snapped noisily in the grate and an explosion of sparks discharged up the chimney.

Then Garrett appeared in the doorway. "What the devil is going on in here?" he asked. "I heard shouting."

"No one is shouting," Adelaide replied, holding out her hands to push down the tension in the room. "There has just been a misunderstanding. That is all."

Garrett turned his narrowed gaze toward Drake. "Good evening, sir," he said in a rather threatening tone that caused Charlotte to glance down at Drake's hands again. He was still flexing and squeezing those big brawny fists.

"Good evening," Drake replied. Then, without waiting for an introduction, he strode out of the library, shouldering his way past Garrett. He walked out of the house and slammed the door violently behind him.

Charlotte ran to follow, but Garrett grabbed hold of her arm and held her back. "Let him go," he said.

"But you don't understand! You don't know what has happened."

"I saw the look in his eye," Garrett said. "He was fit to be tied. Is that the boxer?"

"The retired boxer," she clarified. "And yes, that was Mr. Torrington."

Gone now. Walked out of her life—probably for good.

Garrett turned to Adelaide. He glanced at her left hand. "Good Lord, is that a boulder on your finger?"

Charlotte turned to look as well, and despite everything, felt a deep stirring of happiness when her mother lifted her hand.

"William gave it to me tonight," she said. "He has proposed, and I have accepted."

Charlotte and Garrett moved together across the carpet, their footsteps perfectly in sync, and embraced their parents.

"I am so happy for you," Charlotte said. "This is the most wonderful news I could ever hope for."

No more was said about the awkward confrontation with Mr. Torrington, for no one wanted to spoil a precious event that was a long time coming and deserved to be celebrated to the fullest.

 formerlyformerly

Drake burst through the front door of his house and dashed up the stairs.

Bang! Bang! Bang!

With a tight fist, he pounded on his mother's door until it rattled on the hinges. "Open up, Mother!" he shouted. "I must speak with you."

He heard the sounds of the bed creaking and the shuffling of her footsteps across the floor. The door swung open.

"Where have you been?" she asked, her eyes puffy and red.

"I was out seeking answers," Drake replied. "I went to confront Dr. Thomas, only to find him in the company of another woman. Did you know about that?"

She regarded him with a furrowed brow. "I suspected as much and should have known better. He is a dishonorable philanderer, just like your father."

"But what do you know about the other woman?" Drake pressed as he followed her into the room. "Was there an agreement between you and Doctor Thomas? Did he actually propose?"

His mother glared at him with derision. "No. But all the signs were there. He led me to believe—"

"You believed what you *wanted* to believe, Mother. If there was no proposal, there was no promise of anything. Yet you wrote to me in America and asked me to come home to arrange for your future as a married woman. If anyone misled anyone, it was *you*. But that is not the worst of it. I saw Lady Charlotte tonight, and I know it is *her* mother, the Dowager Duchess of Pembroke, who has stolen your alleged fiancé away from you. Charlotte told me what you said to her when she paid a call here this afternoon. Do you know what I am referring to?"

Eyes as wide as saucers, his mother stared at him intensely, then hobbled to the chair before the fire and collapsed into it. "She was the duchess's daughter. I didn't want you to see her anymore."

"Why not?"

She swung her gaze up at him. "Because her mother was my rival! For two years, the dowager remained in the country, and William began to forget her. I like to believe I helped him to finally give her up, but then Lady Charlotte took a stroll down our street and fell victim to a purse thief. If not for that incident, they would not have stayed in London. Fate is cruel beast, Drake! *You*, my only son, are the reason the dowager got in my way. What were the odds? Everyone knows Lady Charlotte is as reclusive as you are, living under the pretense of being a writer."

"There is no pretense," he told her, for he could not stomach the inaccuracy. "Lady Charlotte's work has been published. And very successfully." He would leave it at that.

"Oh, what does it matter?" his mother said. "It is over now. William has cut me from his heart and his life, and I must accept it. I should have known I could never be so fortunate as to have a man like him for a husband. I had such high hopes though. I thought there might be happiness in my future, but my whole existence has been a tragedy from start to finish. Why do I keep hoping?"

Drake's temper cooled and grew quiet as he watched his mother stare miserably into the dancing flames of the hearth.

He had never felt close to her in the past, for his father was always the dominant figure in the house. He overshadowed any affection that could have existed. Drake had been too busy defending himself from beatings, and later, simply withdrawing to the extent of a transatlantic crossing.

But what about his mother, who had remained here at her post, living through the loss of her two daughters and the appalling violent boxing career of her only living son? Drake remembered how he came home night after night—in a wretched state, barely able to stand, spitting blood, his face swollen and bruised, his ribs broken. Mrs. March had always tended to his wounds. The footmen, occasionally, had been required to carry him upstairs to bed.

No wonder his mother had been happy to see him leave the country, knowing he would give up the sport. If one could call boxing a sport in his case.

Yet he had always resented her. Was it time for change?

Slowly, he moved forward and crouched down at her feet. He took both her hands in his and spoke gently. "I am sorry your relationship ended badly. But

I need to know ... What did you say to Lady Charlotte today? You must tell me."

Her mournful eyes lifted. "I'm sorry. I couldn't help myself. It was selfish of me. I won't deny it. I just wanted her to disappear."

He took a few deep breaths. "Did she send a letter? Did you keep it from me?"

She looked down at her lap. "Yes. I burned it."

Drake imagined how pleased he would have been to receive such a letter from Charlotte, a request to join him on the river that morning. He would have been there to pick her up at precisely six o'clock. He would not have been a single moment late.

"She told me you said some unpleasant things to her. Is that true?"

His mother nodded, then bowed her head. "I am ashamed. You should go back to America now and never speak to me again, Drake. I wouldn't blame you for it. God knows I deserve it."

He squeezed her hands. "Your life hasn't been easy, and you deserve happiness, Mother, as we all do. I don't want to leave you, but I *do* want you to do something for me. Can you get dressed?"

Her weary eyes met his, and she cupped his cheek in her hand. "I will do anything for you, Drake, for you are my only son. All I want is your forgiveness. Not just for today, but for all of it. You know what I am talking about."

Yes, he knew.

He kissed her hand. "Of course I will forgive you, Mother, if you will forgive me as well for deserting you and for staying away so long. But please ... I need you to get up and come with me now. Will you do that?"

She nodded and rose to her feet.

Two hours later, Charlotte was slouching low on the sofa in the drawing room, sipping her third glass of Scottish whisky.

Adelaide, William, and Garrett had done their best to cheer her up by inviting her to play cards, but she had no interest in table games, for she just watched the man she loved walk out of her house in a terrible temper with a look of absolute loathing in his eyes.

'You shouldn't meddle in other people's love affairs,' he had once said to her. Little did he know it was his own mother she was scheming against, working to break up the courtship that had no doubt been at the summit of all his mother's hopes and dreams. How could Charlotte blame Mrs. Torrington? William was a handsome and extraordinary man. She must have been madly in love with him.

Charlotte thought about what Adelaide had said earlier—that we must be forgiving, for we could not know what miseries Mrs. Torrington had suffered in her life. But Charlotte *did* know, for Drake had told her things about his childhood. He had lost his sisters to illness and had been raised by a violent, abusive father.

She could only presume that his mother had suffered an equal degree of despair, for she had been married to that violent abuser and had watched both her daughters fall victim to diphtheria. Charlotte tried to imagine what that must have been like. No wonder Drake's mother was angry and controlling—and desperate to have a good man for her own husband.

And Mrs. Torrington had not known that Charlotte was that good man's illegitimate daughter. If she had known, perhaps she would have made an effort to win Charlotte's approval and affections. All she knew was that Charlotte was the daughter of her rival.

She swirled her whisky around in her glass, then tipped it up and swallowed the entire contents in a single gulp.

The others were quietly playing cards, glancing over at her occasionally with concern. Her head was in a fog. All she wanted to do was keel over sideways and fall asleep right here on the sofa cushions.

She was only vaguely aware of the butler entering the drawing room, and was startled when he appeared in front of her. He cleared his throat. Loudly. She strained to lift her heavy-lidded gaze to look up at him.

"You have a visitor, my lady," he said in his deep, authoritative voice. "He is waiting for you in the library."

"Who is it?" she asked, her head swimming and bobbing about.

"Mr. Torrington."

That sobered her up in a hurry. Charlotte blinked a few times and sat forward. "He's here? Now? What does he want?"

"I don't know, my lady."

She became aware, suddenly, of Garrett, William, and her mother, all staring at her worriedly from the card table.

"I will go and see what he wants," Charlotte said, rising unsteadily to her feet. She wobbled slightly.

"Perhaps I should go with you," Garrett said.

"That is not necessary," she insisted, raising a hand to object. "I am perfectly capable of . . ."

What? Descending the stairs without tumbling to the bottom and falling on her face? Not a certainty ... Oh, she shouldn't have poured that third glass of whisky. Now she was pickled.

But she had no choice. She had to go down there and see him. In all honesty, she wanted to see him, for she had been crushed by his sudden departure and the fact that he blamed her for his mother's misery.

It was, unquestionably, all her fault. If she hadn't sent that letter to William assuring him of his success with Adelaide, perhaps he would still be at the theater with Mrs. Torrington tonight and none of this would have happened.

But would that have been preferable? No, it most certainly would not, for one of her lifelong prayers had been answered tonight. Her mother was engaged to marry Dr. William Thomas, the great love of her life. How could Charlotte wish for anything different?

A few moments later, she was walking into the library, marveling at the fact that she was standing in the same room with Mr. Torrington, when a short while ago, she had fully accepted and believed she would never lay eyes on him again. But here he was. In the flesh. Like a gorgeous Greek god before her. So handsome and appealing. Her body ached to touch him and hold him close. What she wouldn't give to go back to those lazy days at Pembroke, when they were free to make love every night, when she had dared to hope that something more would come of this.

"Mr. Torrington," she said. "I didn't expect you to return."

He was looking down, holding his hat in his hands, turning it over and over. "How could I stay away," he replied, "when I could not bear the thought of your disdain?"

Charlotte frowned in confusion. "It is you who walked out, sir, and I saw the loathing in your eyes. The disdain was in your camp, not mine."

At last he looked up and met her eyes with a look of intense dismay. "Yes, but that loathing was not directed at *you*." He approached her and held out his hand. "You must come outside with me."

"Why?"

"There is something you need to hear."

For better or worse, Charlotte trusted him completely and laid her hand in his. He led her out of the library, across the entrance hall, and out the front door.

It was a warm summer night and crickets were chirping in the square. Charlotte felt the effects of the whisky fading, for she was acutely aware of every sound and sensation—the tap of Drake's footsteps down the cement steps, and the warm touch of his hand.

His coach was parked out front. He opened the door and gestured for her to climb inside. She did so without hesitation, not knowing what he intended. But she would go with him anywhere, willingly, even though she still believed he was angry with her for unwittingly meddling in his mother's affairs.

Charlotte sat down on the upholstered seat and was surprised to discover another occupant in the dimly lit interior—Drake's mother, Mrs. Torrington.

Drake climbed in and sat beside Charlotte, who straightened her posture and prepared herself for another verbal lashing from this woman who must surely despise her, now more than ever.

"Good evening, Lady Charlotte," Mrs. Torrington said.

"Good evening," Charlotte coolly replied.

The tension was thicker than turtle soup.

Drake said nothing for the longest time, and Charlotte wondered why he had brought her here. To punish her further?

"Mother ..." he said in a deep voice edged with command.

Mrs. Torrington took in a deep breath at the sound of his urging, and cleared her throat. "I have come to apologize to you, Lady Charlotte. My behavior this afternoon was inexcusable, and I was wrong to say all the things I did. I must also apologize for reading the letter you sent to my son, which arrived yesterday. I took it and hid it from him. I burned it, in fact. He did not know you had returned to London, and he did not receive your request to join him on the river this morning. He never knew."

Charlotte sat very still while she pondered Mrs. Torrington's apology and confession.

According to his mother, Drake never received her letter, so Charlotte had been correct to give him the benefit of the doubt. But still, there were so many cruel words spoken in this woman's parlor that afternoon ...

Then Charlotte thought of Adelaide's wise words again, and her own knowledge of the life this woman had led. She strove to seek a deeper understanding.

"Why did you not want me to be with your son?" she asked. "I care for him deeply."

Drake's hand came to rest upon hers, and she turned her head to look into his eyes.

"I care for you as well," he said, "and I have made that exceedingly clear to my mother this evening."

Charlotte's gaze darted back to Mrs. Torrington, who sat across from them.

"I cannot possibly express how sorry I am," she said. "I was selfish and I was thinking only of myself."

"Tell her why," Drake said, nudging her further when she hesitated.

Mrs. Torrington raised a handkerchief to her eyes and dabbed at the corners. "I didn't want you in my son's life because I knew whose daughter you were—Adelaide Sinclair's, the Dowager Duchess of Pembroke, William's true beloved. I knew that William loved her and I resented you because you brought her back to London. I wanted you and your mother to go away. I wanted William for myself, for he is the most wonderful man I ever met."

Charlotte watched Mrs. Torrington in the flickering light from the carriage lamp and felt quite certain there was genuine remorse in her heart, and a hint of shame as well, for Mrs. Torrington had tried to come between her son and a woman who truly loved him.

"Can you ever forgive me?" Mrs. Torrington asked.

Charlotte felt all the tension and misery drain out of her body, and took great care in searching for the right words.

"Of course I can," she said, "for you have been very kind to me this evening. You have brought your son back into my life, and you have eased my soul. To think that he never received my letter about joining him on the river this morning ... I thought perhaps he was making me wait intentionally, so I'd understand he wished to be rid of me."

"I am sure he would have come for you," she said, "if he had known you were waiting."

"Yes, I would." Drake leaned close and kissed Charlotte on the forehead. Her heart swelled with love.

"I couldn't stay away from you," Charlotte whispered. "I had to come back to London so that I could tell you how I felt."

"If you hadn't come," he said, "I would have taken the train to Pembroke tomorrow, for I felt the same way. I cannot bear to be without you."

She closed her eyes and rested her forehead on his shoulder, while they all sat in silence.

"You should go home now, Mother," he said, "but I must stay to have a word with Dr. Thomas. You can send the coach back for me."

He and Charlotte exited the vehicle, but before they made their way back to the house, Mrs. Torrington leaned out the open door.

"Will you do something for me, Lady Charlotte?" she asked.

"Yes. What is it?"

"Will you wish your mother well, and congratulate her on her engagement? Tell her ..." Mrs. Torrington swallowed hard and forced the words out. "Tell her she deserves every happiness. Please extend my good wishes and felicitations to Dr. Thomas as well."

"I will do that," Charlotte replied with a smile. "Thank you, Mrs. Torrington. That is very kind."

Drake's mother smiled in return, but it was colored with melancholy. Her eyes brimmed with tears she fought to hold back as she closed the door.

Charlotte vowed to visit Mrs. Torrington the following day and bring her some fresh flowers, for she was well acquainted with the heartache the woman would endure over the coming weeks. Charlotte also understood the importance of friendship at such a time. She would do what she could to bring some cheer to Mrs. Torrington's life. Perhaps in time, Charlotte might even put her matchmaking skills to good use again, for she knew more than a few eligible bachelors of an appropriate age ...

The coach pulled away from the curb. Charlotte turned to face Drake in the dim light that filtered out from the windows of Pembroke House. "You mentioned you wanted to speak with Dr. Thomas," she said. "I hope you don't intend to challenge him to a duel, or heaven forbid, a boxing match, for breaking your mother's heart."

Drake chuckled and shook his head. "No, my darling. I wish only to apologize to him for my behavior earlier. I understand that he has loved your mother for an eternity, and I cannot begrudge him for being honest with mine. He did the honorable thing to end it now and follow his heart, for a man must be with the woman he loves. He cannot let anything stand in his way. But there is more I wish to say to him. Or rather, to *ask* him, if you will allow it."

There on the sidewalk, Drake dropped down on one knee before her and reached into his pocket. "I am in love with you, Charlotte, and I cannot imagine living another day without you in my life." He pulled out a glittering diamond ring and showed it to her. "I need to know that you will always be at my side, and in my bed. I don't care where we live—here or across the Atlantic—as long as we are together. And I will consider myself privileged to take you to parties and balls and dance with you until dawn. I want the whole world to know you are mine, for you have brought peace and happiness back into my life. So please permit me to ask this important question. Will you marry me?"

Charlotte covered her mouth with a hand and hiccupped. "Yes, I will!"

His eyes smiled first, then his faced warmed into an expression of pure joy and relief. He stood up and took hold of her hand. "May I put this on you?"

"Please."

Her fingers trembled as he slipped the ring onto her finger. It fit perfectly.

"It's beautiful, Drake. I am so happy I could cry. But when did you decide this?"

"I knew I loved you at Pembroke," he explained, "in the forest, when you stood in the rain at sunset. You were the most beautiful vision imaginable. That was the moment you had my heart forever." Pulling her into his strong muscled arms, he held her tight. "Will your father give us his blessing?"

"Is that what you wanted to ask him?"

"Yes."

"Well, I don't see a problem, for he knows true love when he sees it, and he knows it lasts forever."

She felt the bond between them spark into a red-hot flame as his lips found hers and his hands slid around her waist. The kiss was demanding and passionate and sent her heart spinning into a breathtaking world of pleasure and joy. He kissed her hard until she feared her knees might buckle and she might faint there in his arms.

He pulled back and smiled down at her, his silvery eyes glimmering in the moonlight.

"Good Lord, you taste like a brewery," he said. "Are you drunk, my darling?"

"Drunk with love," she replied with a grin.

He laughed. "You're going to feel miserable in the morning."

"There is no chance of that," she said, shaking her head, "for I will be too busy feeling grateful—grateful for the fact that I was attacked by a purse thief this summer and bashed on the head. How lucky I was that day."

"And how lucky I am on *this* day," he replied. "I will thank the heavens for bring you into my life ... until the day I die." Then he covered her mouth again in a soul-reaching kiss that lifted her clear off the ground.

Epilogue

*I*N THE AUTUMN OF that year, two family weddings took place at the chapel at Pembroke Palace. First, in September, the dowager duchess, at the youthful age of sixty-two, walked down the aisle in the presence of all her children and grandchildren, to marry the man she had known and loved her entire life—the renowned surgeon, Dr. William Thomas. They made plans to travel to America together the following summer to visit the Grand Canyon.

In October, when the leaves were changing and the air was crisp, the chapel bells rang yet again to celebrate the nuptials of Lady Charlotte Sinclair, who was also known, to those close to her, as reclusive bestselling author Victor Edwards.

Charlotte was anything but reclusive, however, for she and her new husband, Drake Torrington, began a honeymoon and world tour that lasted two spectacular years. They followed in the footsteps of her older brother Lord Vincent, who had traveled to Egypt and India with his new bride over a decade earlier. After visiting the pyramids and climbing Mount Vesuvius in Italy, Charlotte and Drake boarded a luxurious steamship bound for America and crossed the Atlantic.

For a full year they resided in the city of Boston, where Drake won three prestigious rowing trophies and invested heavily in a small, unknown company that was perfecting the art of refrigeration. By the turn of the century, he and Lady Charlotte were recognized as the wealthiest couple in England, outshining even the Duke of Pembroke himself—who had also invested in the same refrigeration company upon the advice of his brother-in-law, Mr. Torrington.

By that time, Lady Charlotte had given birth to two children and had written five more novels, each one more successful and critically acclaimed than the last. Not long after the death of Queen Victoria, however, Victor Edwards's true identity was discovered, and Charlotte became a notorious literary figure, who, nevertheless continued to write under her famous pen name.

She also enjoyed the success of her matchmaking talents, for on her wedding day, she introduced Drake's mother to a kind-hearted viscount from Devonshire. One year later they were married.

Back at Pembroke Palace, the next generation of Sinclairs entered the London marriage mart, and one-by-one, they all married for love, just like their parents.

The Pembroke Palace curse had been thwarted. In fact, no one remembered much about it when motor cars and electric lights invaded the quiet stillness of the Old World. It was rarely spoken of, although the subterranean passages continued to arouse gossip whenever the young people ventured below during a house party. Sometimes they emerged with stories of dead monks who appeared like mist before their eyes and frightened the ladies into the gentlemen's arms. The catacombs were the perfect destination for stolen kisses and new courtships, which resulted in more than a few hasty, unexpected marriages over the years.

Happily, Adelaide, the dowager duchess, and her husband Dr. William Thomas, enjoyed a long and loving marriage. The duchess became the beloved great-great-grandmother to a whole new generation of Sinclairs and reached the ripe old age of ninety-two before she passed away in 1916. Dr. Thomas passed away one week later, proving yet again that he would never leave her side.

Eternal love. It was a common theme at Pembroke Palace. All who lived there were loved to the highest degree, and to everyone's delight, those blessings never ceased.

ᘐᘜᘔ

Dear Reader,

I hope you enjoyed Charlotte and Drake's story, which brings the Pembroke Palace series to a happy conclusion at the end of the Victorian era.

Please let me know if you enjoyed the series and would like to see it continue. I was sorry to say good-bye to these characters, with whom I spent so much time, and would enjoy venturing into the Edwardian era to revisit the next generation, if that interests you.

You can contact me through my website, and please sign up for my mailing list so I can keep you informed about all my upcoming releases.

In the meantime I have included information about the other books in the Pembroke Palace series.

Thank you again for taking the time to read SEDUCED AT SUNSET, and I hope you enjoy many more hours of pleasurable reading in the romance genre!

All my best,
Julianne

Pembroke Palace Series Book One
IN MY WILDEST FANTASIES
Available from Avon/Harper Collins

Four years ago, a mesmerizing stranger pulled Lady Rebecca Newland from her runaway coach, galloping to her rescue in a fog-shrouded forest. Though she was just seventeen, Rebecca felt an irresistible desire for the mysterious man and swore that she would someday be his bride. But now she is betrothed to another man whom she detests—and Devon Sinclair, the future Duke of Pembroke and her hero, lies tantalizingly beyond her reach . . .

Haunted by an unspeakable past, Devon has no intention of taking a wife, not even the enticing Rebecca. But then his father rules that Devon must wed by Christmas or forfeit his rightful inheritance. Now, with his fortune at stake, Devon sets out to lure Rebecca to his bed . . . where the most unexpected secrets and lies stand in the way of their scandalous, explosive passion.

Pembroke Palace Series Book Two
THE MISTRESS DIARIES
Available from Avon/Harper Collins

He told me he would treat my heart with great care. He was lying of course, for it was all a very clever, skillful seduction ...

The night I met Lord Vincent Sinclair, son of the Duke of Pembroke, was the night I lost control. I never imagined that I, Cassandra Montrose, could engage in such wicked, wanton behavior with a man I hardly knew. But in that fateful moment, alone in his coach, the passion I felt for him was undeniable, even though I knew that after my surrender I was unlikely to ever see my lover again. Until a fateful secret brought me to his door ...

I always believed my pride would prevent me from becoming any man's mistress—especially a rogue like Vincent, who cares for nothing but his inheritance. Yet I have very good reason to remain in his life. If only he did not tempt me so ...

Pembroke Palace Series Book Three
WHEN A STRANGER LOVES ME
Available from Avon/Harper Collins

I saved his life, and I had much to demand in return ...

When he washed up on shore, I knew my prayers had been answered, and that I, Lady Chelsea Campion, need no longer fear poverty and heartbreak. To secure my family's estate, all I needed was a child. Handsome, clearly noble-born, and with no memory of his previous life, the mysterious man was perfect. All I had to do was visit his bedchamber and seduce him.

I had expected him to be a skillful, scandalously wonderful lover, but once in his arms I was overcome by something more than mere passion. I had fallen hopelessly, desperately in love.

My plan has now gone shockingly awry. But I will not give up a man who makes me feel such wicked ecstasy. No matter his true identity, no matter the secrets he struggles to remember, I will do anything in this world to make this stranger love me ...

Pembroke Palace Series Book Four
MARRIED BY MIDNIGHT
Available Now

AN UNATTAINABLE ROGUE ...

For seven years, Lord Garrett Sinclair—the ruggedly handsome illegitimate son of the Duke of Pembroke—has been traveling abroad with no intention of ever returning home to Pembroke Palace ... until his father commands that he must marry by Christmas in order to thwart a family curse or lose his inheritance forever. Haunted by a tragic accident that has hardened his soul, Garrett entrusts his brothers to seek out a bride who will agree to a marriage in name only. Her reward? A sizable share of his inheritance—payable immediately after the wedding night ....

A BEAUTIFUL TEMPTRESS ...

Lady Anne Douglas has been ruined by scandal and disowned by her father. Facing a life of poverty and spinsterhood, she leaps at the generous terms of the marriage contract to ensure her independence. But the charade of a two-week engagement proves more of a challenge than either anticipated when they cannot resist the intoxicating lure of the marriage bed. Anne knows they will part ways after the wedding. Will she dare risk her heart for two weeks of pleasure in the arms of an irresistible rogue? Or will her surrender become her undoing after a most unexpected turn of events mere hours before the wedding?

Books by Julianne MacLean

The American Heiress Series
Published by Avon/Harper Collins:
To Marry the Duke
An Affair Most Wicked
My Own Private Hero
Love According to Lily
Portrait of a Lover
Surrender to a Scoundrel

The Pembroke Palace Series
Published by Avon/Harper Collins:
In My Wildest Fantasies
The Mistress Diaries
When a Stranger Loves Me
Married By Midnight
A Kiss Before the Wedding - A
Pembroke Palace Short Story
Seduced at Sunset

The Highlander Trilogy
Published by St. Martin's Press:
Captured by the Highlander
Claimed by the Highlander
Seduced by the Highlander
The Rebel – A Highland Short Story

The Royal Trilogy
Published by St. Martin's Press:
Be My Prince
Princess in Love
The Prince's Bride

Harlequin Historical Romances:
Prairie Bride
The Marshal and Mrs. O'Malley
Adam's Promise

Time Travel Romance
Taken by the Cowboy

Contemporary Fiction:
The Color of Heaven
The Color of Destiny
The Color of Hope

About the Author

Julianne MacLean is a *USA Today* bestselling author of numerous historical romances, including The Highlander Trilogy with St. Martin's Press and her popular American Heiress Series with Avon/Harper Collins. She also writes contemporary mainstream fiction, and her recent release The Color of Heaven was a *USA Today* bestseller. She is a three-time RITA finalist, and has won numerous awards, including the Booksellers' Best Award, the Book Buyer's Best Award, and a Reviewers' Choice Award from Romantic Times for Best Regency Historical of 2005. She lives in Nova Scotia with her husband and daughter, and is a dedicated member of Romance Writers of Atlantic Canada. Please visit Julianne's website at www. juliannemaclean.com for more information about her novels, and to enter for a chance to win her monthly autographed book giveaway.

CPSIA information can be obtained
at www.ICGtesting.com
Printed in the USA
LVOW12s1223210816

501252LV00001B/30/P